With best wishes!

Lesley Ann Croston

Here's what people are saying:

"I'm so glad Lesley wrote <u>Moonlight In Jungleland</u>. I laughed like I used to laugh in sixth grade. It's such a gift to be so clearly reminded of the zany humor, creativity, and courage it takes to grow up female."
—**Marcy Lund,** Owner - Café Olga

"I loved <u>Moonlight In Jungleland</u>. I didn't want it to end. "
—**Pat MacDonald,** Carpenter

"It was a return to innocence. I read parts of <u>Moonlight In Jungleland</u> to a friend and we just laughed, and laughed, and laughed. "
—**Anne Pekuri,** Writer

"I've just finished reading <u>Moonlight In Jungleland</u> and I'm about ready to organize a fan club..."
—**Sidney Raffel, M.D.**

"The growing up years recalled with humor and honesty. <u>Moonlight In Jungleland</u> can be read with pleasure regardless of your age."
—**Margaret Philbrick,** Pianist

"What I want to know is - where's the sequel?"
—**Lawrence Allen,** retired
Shipyard Manager

"<u>Moonlight In Jungleland</u> is a wonderful tale. I laughed, and I cried, transported by Lesley's high-spirited adventures."
— **Magda Mische, N.D.**

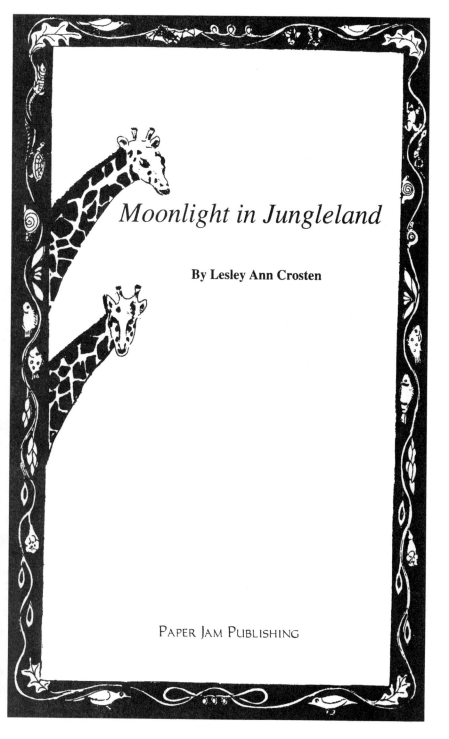

Moonlight in Jungleland

By Lesley Ann Crosten

PAPER JAM PUBLISHING

Published by
PAPER JAM PUBLISHING, LLP
Post Office Box 435
Eastsound, WA 98245

Library of Congress Number 96-70959
ISBN 1-888345-03-9
Third Edition

For Cynthia,
a toast to childhood friendship, with all the exuberance
and all the love that disregards convention and outlives
the passages of time and place.

<u>Acknowledgments</u>

I would like to thank Mary and Loran Crosten for their ongoing love and for their enthusiastic support of <u>Moonlight in Jungleland</u>; the entire Raffel family for being eternal best friends; Deanna Shaide for her encouragement and unwavering faith and help; proof readers and advocates Doris Brain, Tom and Evelyn Rodrique, and Margaret Philbrick; Eileen Dean, Tom Tillman, and Linda Kinney-McNulty of Paper Jam Publishing Co. for generous professional help just when I needed it; and lastly I want to thank all the fine spirited people of this island who have consistently made it possible for me to flourish.

Moonlight in Jungleland

By Lesley Ann Crosten

What Next

I was wintering in Los Angeles. This is equivalent to vacationing on Mars or the Salt Flats of Utah if you have been living on a small green island in the Puget Sound. I was sinking into the middle years of my life in a state of stubborn and apparently useless confusion, dashed hopes, and despondency, when I heard from my mother that Cynthia, my best friend from childhood, was diagnosed with breast cancer.

My initial feeling was of disbelief. A shocking horror crept over me as though it were myself silently and malevolently invaded. Then I became outraged. And that is why, after a ten year silence, I telephoned her.

When she answered, I said bluntly,

"Cynthia, you CREEP! How DARE you have cancer?"

She laughed, unhinged. She said it was the first time anyone had treated her and her frightening situation with disrespect. It was a silly relief.

We decided that I would take the earliest flight to Washington D.C. to be with her. The depth of our childhood friendship stood us well, kept us from awkwardness at the lapse of years. In the few weeks I stayed, we reminisced and managed to laugh a lot over all the goofy times we'd enjoyed together. We both perceived the blessing that came through our joining up as loyal partners way back in fifth grade - best friends standing sturdily together in the face of all the pitfalls along the adolescent trail.

Now it was as if we were in a small boat adrift at sea, and Cynthia was hurt. This time I was an adult, yet my ability to help her was limited, even my heart felt too small to love her enough. Then it came to me poignantly one evening, after a chemotherapy session caused her hair to fall out in clumps, that her precious life contained my own. We had *built* our childhoods together, we were irreplaceable to one another. Though we had separated and now lived far apart, we still shared the cherished best times of our childhood - not like siblings born into the same household - but by conscious choice. We had *chosen* to grow up together.

Destiny

Cynthia had long, straight black hair, like an Eskimo, I thought admiringly, which she wore in two thick braids. She had a pleasant oval face, brown eyes, a stubby nose, was shorter than I and slightly plump. In temperament she was good natured through and through. An occasional direct confrontation with spiders caused her to become hysterical, to grab her hair and shriek, yet in other matters she was not especially squeamish. She wore casual hand-me-downs, knee-length flared skirts which she herself ironed, short-sleeved teeshirts and sandals. Most mornings she made and served her mother and father coffee in bed before she went to school. And she had every intention of becoming a nurse when she grew up, just like her mother. Cynthia was my absolutely best friend from the time we first sat next to each other in fifth grade. It was destiny.

Cynthia belonged to a family with five girls, all fairly close in age. She was the fourth child. Both parents were very loving and devoted to the family. Not a great amount of attention was given to any particular child, but there was always a prevailing air of generosity and welcomeness. Parties and celebrations occurred regularly and relatives abounded. Food was plentiful; everyone seemed happy and secure.

Unlike Cynthia, I had freckles and cropped reddish hair, was on the lean side, and especially agile. In my early years I excelled at shinnying up flagpoles and hanging languidly upside down on the monkey bars for the entire recess period. By fourth grade I was a nimble sprinter. I fancied myself a fleet footed warrior, and supposed that in some great sacrificial deed I would be hunted down, imprisoned, burned at the stake or mercilessly shot in a place like the O.K. Corral, to everyone's horror, amazement and endless sorrow; afterwards of course being fussed over and raised to Sainthood much like Joan of Arc. Mother said my imagination worked overtime.

In September of fifth grade Cynthia was new to the neighborhood and our campus elementary school. She did not know what to expect and she was nervous. I was equally insecure. My family and I were just returning to northern California after a year in France, where my brother and I had been separated from our parents and placed in a French boarding home. I had missed my mother terribly. At bedtime I often sobbed myself to sleep. I had the gnawing suspicion that Stephen and I were no longer wanted and that Mother and Father might not come back for us. It was a severely frightening time, one that would separate me under the surface from other girls my age; one that would complicate my outlook.

Deep emotional fear can cause a person to become fragile, like an old water pipe with invisible cracks at every joint. It looks perfectly normal until there is a little pressure, and then springs leaks everywhere.

I was fragile upon entering fifth grade even though I may have looked normal. I had very little confidence left. And there was Cynthia sitting next to me in a radiantly warm and cozy glow. Destiny.

There are certain intuitive knowings that occur in our

4

lives on special occasions. She was without doubt a positively clear signal to me of the end of my troubled times. Not that I could have told you why; I just knew it. Cynthia, uneasy and lonely herself, welcomed my enthusiastic smile with obvious relief.

"Hi," she said pleasantly. "I'm Cynthia."

"And I'm Lesley!" I said in a happy rush. "Want some of my orange?" I pointed to the bulge in my pocket. "I picked it offa Mr. Brand's tree on the way to school - it'll be real juicy and delicious!"

"Oh boy!" Cynthia replied, "I love oranges!"

I could feel a prickle of pleasure - my secret indication that this was the beginning of a very compatible association. Already we had something important in common: we both loved oranges! By lunch time we had figured out where we each lived and agreed to walk home together so that I could show her Mr. Brand's wonderful orange trees, and Mrs. Moser's tortoise. Life was once again full of promise and a lot safer.

Our fathers were professors at Stanford and we both lived in the old neighborhood on campus, minutes away from one another along a shady, meandering country lane that even had a stream crossing it with a white picket fence. This became our special meeting place because it was secluded and notably romantic. We walked home together that first day and each day thereafter in profound contentment on pathways that led past walnut trees, tangerine trees, fig trees and loquat trees. We lived in a veritable garden of Eden, exploring and claiming it all, only occasionally being run off by an irate and territorial professor.

There were several alternate paths we took depending on the mood and season. There was, for instance, the long curving sidewalk that led past the "maple syrup bush", which was worth passing several times for the delicious whiff, or there was the more tangled narrow footpath that led through several neighbor yards, one with a kumquat tree and pineapple guavas and luscious oranges and many fragrant old-fashioned roses, and one with a breath-taking slide made just for neighborhood children, and an ancient tortoise that lived under a rock and ate lettuce. The woman who inhabited the house on this property was elderly and mad. She looked like a witchy wraith, perhaps because her long grey hair hung about her shoulders and she wore her tattered nightgown during the day. The possibility of seeing her excited us.

On the way home Cynthia was full of superstitions. I happily adopted them all. Out of respect for our mothers, and their backs in particular, we were careful to step over all cracks in the sidewalk, to say "bread and butter" if we went on opposite sides of a lamp post, to throw salt over our left shoulders if we spilled any out of our lunch boxes, and to knock on wood when we mentioned our good fortune. We wished on the first star every evening, and yelled "Pediddle!" if we ever saw a car with only one bright headlight.

When we arrived at Cynthia's big Tudor house with its terraced gardens, we hopefully found banana-chocolate-ripple-butterscotch-fudge ice-cream, our all-time favorite, fancy large olives with pimentos, and french bread with pale yellow dollops of sweet butter. After foraging through Cynthia's kitchen we ambled, barefoot by now, to my modern ranch style house located in an orchard where there was both a pomegranate tree and a persimmon tree, and a yard full of apple and plum trees. Once we got to the kitchen, we cooked up a few Swedish pancakes, which consisted of four eggs mixed with flour and milk and stuffed with bacon and marmalade. After being served them once by Cynthia's mother, I figured out how to cook

them for Cynthia and me on a near daily basis. The
pancakes were followed by a large bowl of popcorn with
lemonade chasers on the side. Lastly, bulging and satisfied, we generally flopped down to watch reruns of "Our
Gang" comedies, or danced in our underwear to Strauss
waltzes on the old Victrola.

Sanctuary

In spite of this budding friendship with Cynthia, I often needed to be by myself. Living back in my own home was all that I wished for, yet it was strange and emotionally congested. I no longer took home for granted like other kids and I was secretly suspicious of not being wanted as much as other kids whose families and activities were child centered. I once heard that "children of lovers are orphans. " My parents fell in love the night they met, and spent their married lives as lovers of one another first and foremost. My brother and I were never central to the marriage as in most families. Rather we were satellites revolving around the union of my parents. Stephen, who had been my closest touch to family in France, became a tease at home. Before long I decided to build myself a separate dwelling behind the woodpile. We had some old wooden planks stored out back, and I worked hard, enlisting my mother's and brother's reluctant help to erect a seven foot square shack with windows and a hinged door. All the nails were second hand, straightened out from a previous building project. When the shack was completed I even put in a tiny front yard with a picket fence. My shack could not be seen from the house and was well hidden by an almond tree. It was a great solace. I constructed crude little stools and a small cupboard, and nailed up a pair of hammocks made from old blankets. Then I stood back and marvelled because I had created my first sanctuary.

Eventually I invited Cynthia over to spend the night with me in the shack. She was joyful and willing, and life that year would not have been complete or even marginally satisfactory without her wonderful friendship. Although it is true that I initiated most of our projects, Cynthia embellished them with color and detail and her very presence made them seem worthwhile. Those projects that did not reach completion failed only because we lacked financing, expertise, or were sabotaged by certain other persons. I hate to point a finger, but it is a fact that Stephen and his then constant companion, Peter, were not opposed to sabotage and even practiced it as an art form in their spare moments. Stephen preyed on us relentlessly as soon as the shack was complete. The fact that I had my own private dwelling drove him crazy. A favorite prank of his was to sneak in and sever all but a few strands of the ends of the hammocks attached to the wall so that Cynthia and I could get comfortably settled, but after a few moments our weight would cause the remaining strands to break, and we would dump clumsily onto the floor. The sound of our misfortune pleasured him no end. We could even hear his barely suppressed giggles on the other side of the wall.

Stephen tormented us until the day he closed the door to his room, pulled the curtains, and then could be heard but not seen for several days. The noises coming from his room were spirited and industrious. Finally late one afternoon he emerged. His room glowed with burgundy lights. He had made it into a miniature casino. There was a poster of a sultry woman tacked to the ceiling looking down over Stephen's extravaganza. The room was such a

9

breath stopping vision, such an enticing gambling den that mother and father incorporated it, and Stephen, into their forthcoming faculty party. They made the whole house into a fanciful Monte Carlo Casino. At the front door guests were given two hundred dollars of play money which they could exchange for chips to play the games in Stephen's room. From the excited chatter and bustle throughout the evening I judged it one of our most successful parties. Stephen and Peter presided over the affair as hosts, celebrities, and entrepreneurs. They wore black satin vests and red bow ties and they were obviously pleased with themselves.

Summertime

Every year, when summer came my family travelled by train or car from California to upstate New York. This was a seasonal migration and in early spring the urge to travel would begin to prick at each of us until school's end in early June. We would then without delay pack up and be gone before sun up. The trip across country was long, arduous, and expensive, yet necessary for our spiritual well-being as a family. Mother and Father had found their private Shangri La in the first years of their marriage in the tiny hamlet of Boonville at the foot of the Adirondack Mountains.

Boonville's rolling, rock strewn countryside is not especially fertile, but it is extraordinarily beautiful. Meandering through its pastoral valleys and forest lands are three rivers: the Black River, the Moose River, and the Dry Sugar River. The Black River is a friendly, familiar river that runs through the open farm lands, with many good fishing holes, rapids, and summer camps dotting its shores. The Moose River is fierce and comes through more rugged terrain, cascading over granite boulders and rushing through vast canyons that it has created over time. The Dry Sugar spends much of its journey underground, emerging here and there in a farmer's pasture and forming ancient, deep shale pools perfect for crawdads and inquisitive exploration.

We swam in all three rivers in our favorite water holes, often bringing picnics, fishing poles for ourselves, oil paints and an easel for Mother. We roamed pastures and woodlands, finding abandoned farms and cabins on the lesser travelled sandy roads. Over the years we came across furnished but derelict hotels and mills along the Moose River. It was fascinating to explore these ruins, and we often came home with treasures. Once we found a working slot machine under the rubble of an old hotel, and a pair of wooden telephones. Mother's booty was usually a small pile of smooth river rocks. As she explored the slippery shores she would drop a favorite rock down the front of her bathing suit in order to keep her hands free for balancing and swimming. She looked pretty funny by the end of an excursion and her bathing suit lost its shape early in the season. Occasionally we required tetanus shots from stepping on rusty nails. Going for an outing always suggested the potential for a major discovery of some lost civilization. The countryside was eerie and nostalgic, holding many hidden memories of once prosperous times. I often felt on the verge of a sudden romantic awakening and at the same time a little melancholy, as though the air carried fragrantly elusive promises meant especially for me, and a memory...

When we went to the Moose River we carried old coffee tins to fill with tart, plump huckleberries and from these Mother made juicy pies. We stuffed cucumber sandwiches with the spicy watercress which grew ankle deep in the bogs of rock strewn cow pastures. Everything smelled edible or tasted and felt excitingly familiar and close to the earth - even the moist air gave away the scent of all the lushly growing green plants.

Poets have waded through Boonville's burbling golden hued brooks and dreamed under ancient sugar maples while black and white spotted cows nibbled at meadow grasses nearby. Downy Milkweed grows along the narrow country lanes, and wild grape tangles itself through bent, rusty wire fences. Whippoorwills serenade on the rooftop every night in summer, and violent thunder and lightning storms sweep over the countryside splitting trees and mining that prehistoric fear deep within us that suddenly one of us shall be selected and struck dead. Storms are best peeked at from under an old familiar blanket on the porch swing.

My parents went to Boonville by train one summer, shortly after getting married, when they had little money and nothing better to do. At the time they were living and working in New York City and had become friends with a frail but vivacious young woman named Jessie Layng. She rented a flat down the hall from them, and she convinced them that they should come home with her for the summer. So they all took the train to Boonville where Jessie's parents met them, took all three home, and then helped mother and father find a place of their own. The year was 1938.

Mother and father rented a small cottage along the Black River, and friendly farmers gave them milk, eggs, fresh vegetables and an occasional chicken. They rented a pair of brand new bicycles from the local hardware store for one dollar. My father was a pianist but he dearly loved to fish; my mother was a painter and she painted everything she saw while father fished. They lived the good life, falling so deeply in love with the country and the local people that, like swallows, they returned every summer thereafter to nest, to greet old friends, to reconnect as a family, and to remember for a few months each year to live the simple, good life.

In l945, when my father was still in the navy, my mother, holding my two year old brother's hand, went to Boonville for sanctuary. She was six months pregnant. She rented a house in town and waited for my father to be released from the navy. Both my father and I were due on Christmas day. Mother could not imagine being laid up on my father's arrival, so eleven days before Christmas she took quinine and epsom salts. I was therefore ten days old when Father and Mother were reunited.

I grew up believing I was born in heaven. Summer months in Boonville were spent hiking, fishing for perch, trout, and bass in the Black River, swimming everyday in the fresh deep waters of the Black River, picking berries, reading old novels from the village library, and day dreaming. Evenings were often enjoyed with friends who came out for highly competitive croquet games, dinners of corn on the cob, grilled chicken, huge fresh salads, followed by berries and cream for dessert. Noisy card games often went on until late in the evening.

Old Timers

Jessie's mother, Hildegarde, was a slender, elegant French woman whose father was a Baron. She talked with a French accent and seemed to be, after many years in this country, still a baroness in exile. She was married to a hard working, gentle local man named Clark. Their marriage was not wildly exciting or one of intimate companionship, for which I believe she yearned, but it was devoted and loyal in its own way. Their only child, Jessie, was the center of Clark's world. She was born frail with congenital arthritis. Hildegarde often told us how much she had wanted a boy and was disappointed at Jessie's birth. Back in France girl children were not appreciated. Hilda had been removed from her own mother and taken to be raised by a wet nurse She therefore had little interest in girls or knowledge of motherhood. This fact caused Jessie to lean to her father for love and nurturing. When she had to go many times to the hospital in Boston, it was Clark who accompanied her and stayed by her bedside. Clark would do anything for Jessie. He was *always* there for her.

Clark owned a saddle and harness shop in Boonville that he later turned into a furniture store when automobiles edged out the horse trade. During the depression a young man from up north came through on the railway. He was an honest, clean living fellow and Clark hired him to work at the store. John was not educated beyond high school but he was very bright and played a jazzy clarinet. He and Jessie eventually fell in love, got married and moved into a fine two story house that Clark built for them.

Village friends included the local banker George, an honest soul who smoked big cigars and whose heart melted over his carefully tended rose garden, and his wife Susan, the village librarian. She was a terrific cook and a woman both strong willed and big hearted. There were local farmers such as old Gramp Charbonneau who grew vegetables and had dairy cows, and Grandma Charbonneau who died of undulant fever one sad winter.

My father had several fishing friends who went out with him to catch the "Black River Monster," a wise old trout that was occasionally seen gobbling up a fat worm. It was far too clever to ever get caught. One of these friends was Louie. He lived across the road in a multi-colored shingle shack. He only had a few fingers on each hand from working in the saw mill. I was fascinated at the way the skin puckered around the stumps of his fingers. Most of his teeth were gone, and the ones that were left were mossy and wiggled when he talked. His common law wife Gracie was a slightly built sweet woman who in winter trudged up the hill to light the fires and clean the latrines of the one room school house. She always had a pot of beans with chicken necks and pork lard sitting on the back of their cast iron wood stove. They had an outhouse, a well with hand pump in their front yard from which we got our drinking water, and they had a little short haired dog named Trixie that used to sing in accompaniment to the hymns over the radio on Sunday mornings.

I adored Gracie. She was the only baby sitter I ever loved. Sometimes at bedtime she would look at us and suddenly shove her front teeth out of her mouth and rush after us. This was her "wolf face". I found it just thrilling that she could remove her teeth at will. I wished that I could do the same. It seemed as exciting and forbidden as Louie's stumpy hands. Gracie would pick up our favorite book and read amazing stories from it - totally different from the stories mother read. When I questioned mother about this one night, because she was reading a boring story out of the same book from which Gracie had read a richly entertaining story only the night before, mother explained that Gracie could not actually read and that she was using her imagination to give us her wonderful bedtime stories.

For many summers we lived across from Gracie and Louie along the banks of the Black River. Hawkinsville was a ramshackle neighborhood with just a few dilapidated houses, an old country store, and a derelict saw mill. Stephen and I played with ragged little children from several run down homes, one that had only a dirt floor. Local men were loggers, unemployed, or worked at a nearby chair factory. The families were terribly poor and the men were hard drinkers. There were many children who lived with their mothers in an unpainted semi-abandoned hotel alongside the upper road. The women's teeth were chipped and black. They could be seen smoking together, drinking cokes and chatting on the porch. The children were unkempt and seemed to be the only ones taking care of each other. We played fanciful games of soldiers, cops and robbers, and complicated games of house where it was commonplace to switch genders and roles. We threw ourselves into these games and they lasted, it seemed, for days. Mother was not keen on having us play with the hotel kids, but they were wild and free and we enjoyed their company. We made vast forts in the hay stored in our barn and quit our games only when mother blew her special whistle calling us home.

Willy Canon owned the tiny grocery store across from the old mill, and kept a glass case of penny candies and a freezer of ice-cream sandwiches and creme sicles that made us drool with desire. He was a harsh old grey, crusty man. I thought he was probably Billy Goat Gruff. It was hard to face him in order to buy candy and going to his store with someone else was safer. He had a grizzled donkey out back that looked just like him.

Chamberpots and Thunderstorms

We rented one of the nicer cottages along the river belonging to the Reverend Hosper. It had a player piano and a screened in porch, one of the only flush toilets in the neighborhood, and two tiny rooms upstairs where we slept. I always slept in a cot across from my parents, and I had a potty tucked under the bed because it was too far and too dark to get downstairs to the bathroom at night. Mother and father and I walked up the narrow stairs and through Stephen's little room to get to ours.

One night mother removed the potty from under my bed and told me that I was old enough to go by myself downstairs to the toilet. Therefore in the darkness that same night I had to creep out from under my covers and grope my way through Stephen's room and climb down the stairs. I was barefoot and about three stairs down I stepped on a large rat. It screamed and so did I. The potty was returned to its place under my cot the very next day. About a week later we located the terrible smell in the kitchen. The rat was dead under the icebox. I must have squished its vitals that fateful night.

There were thunderstorms sometimes in the middle of the night which shook me to my bones. I remember hurrying to my father's side of the bed and him making a curved space for me to crawl into against his stomach and how comforting that was. When I was too old to do this, when I could no longer cuddle against my father, it was a passage for me as sorrowful as the day my mother told me I had outgrown my dolls, and then swiftly boxed them up and removed them from my sight forever. Mother believed in survival, and I think she sensed in me a little of what she called a "leaking Lena." She pushed at me to be strong and independent.

I wondered why there were little boys in the neighborhood, but very few little girls. It always seemed to be this way wherever we went. Hawkinsville was no exception. Perhaps one of the reasons was that the little girls in Hawkinsville grew up very fast. Gracie's niece visited for two weeks every summer and she was close to my age. We played together and had good fun until the summer between fifth and sixth grade. She arrived as a mature young woman and we no longer knew what to say to one another. She was dating an army boy and we might as well have been on different planets because I was totally ignorant of her world and she was far beyond my childish one. Mother decided we would have to bring our own friends with us if we wished to have company.

The next year Stephen brought his best friend Peter along to live with us for the whole summer. I was very lonely for my own friends, and of course I missed Cynthia terribly. Her parents were unwilling to let her go three thousand miles away for the summer months, and so we were forced apart summer after summer to write our letters of longing to be together and letters of plans for the coming years. These we wrote almost every day from the time my family left in June until we returned in the fall. They were genuine love letters, letters of vital connection, assuring each of us that we were partners and not alone.

The most difficult part of the trip in the early years was leaving my cat "Bootsie" behind. Later it became just as

20

hard to leave Cynthia. Bootsie's welfare was a source of great anxiety. She was cared for by various housesitters, but she always became scarce and semi-wild until we returned. I loved her dearly and saw myself as her protector, primarily from my brother who fancied himself a great white hunter of the Northern California Savannah. He obsessively hunted and trailed Bootsie as if she were a rare and exotic tigress. Saturday mornings were usually the worst.

"MOTHER!" I yelled angrily, "STEPHEN'S DOING IT AGAIN ! HE'S KILLING BOOTSIE!"

Mother came out of the kitchen to check on the situation. Stephen announced self-righteously to her,

"I'M ONLY making her go up in my new elevator! I'm just HELPING her to get onto the roof!"

"She doesn't WANT to be on the roof and she doesn't want to be IN THAT STUPID BOX ! " I screamed at him.

"MOMMIEEE!" (Wailing hysterically sometimes worked).

Mother quickly came to Bootsie's rescue. "Stephen!" she said sternly, "Let the cat down immediately!"

"FINE!" replied Stephen, peevishly letting go of the rope that held the box suspended in the air through a system of pulleys attached to the limb of a large almond tree next to the kitchen. Down she came, with a pathetic scream and a thud - still inside the box. Grabbing her up in my arms I carried her apologetically to the sanctuary of my bedroom, muttering all the while evil curses on my brother for his endless mischief.

The constant perilous state in which Bootsie found herself caused her to be extremely shy and to use my bedroom window as her entry into the house. I kept her food dish and her water in my room and she slept with me at night and purred me to sleep from the time I was six.

I worried endlessly about her welfare whenever we

were away, wrote the housesitters often about her food and living requirements and extracted promises from them that they would be kind to her. They usually were. Upon our return and my calling her, she would streak out from the bushes and leap into my arms.

Between fifth and sixth grade, upon arriving in Boonville I received the following important document from our kindly house sitter back in California:

Dear Lesley,

Five of them! One grey and black tiger, one long haired soft gray, just like the little mice with rubber tails, except no pink, two like Bootsie, and the last like Bootsie except her left side has four spots on it.

Mrs. McKinney reported to the gardeners that they were under Dr. Soule's potting shed. Then Wednesday morning there they were in Mrs. McKinney's garage. She didn't want them, as she has eight Siamese, which is enough for her. So we brought them to a big wooden box that we put just outside the guest room, by the ping-pong table, and our son Paul is just inside and cares for them dearly. So I don't think we have a worry in the world, as my wife has had kittens many times and I've had them a few times, and as you say, Bootsie is not unacquainted with motherhood.

Signed,
Bosco The Cat-herd.

I immediately wrote Cynthia and asked her to stroll over and have a look. Cynthia obliged, and replied with the following letter:

Howdy ole girl!

I was so happy to hear about Bootsie having babies! I'll go right over and maybe she'll let me see her kitties. Then I might even take pictures of the little putties.

We sure have been living it up! Today we went swimming and the water was freezing but refreshing. I met this girl and she is my age, but don't worry - I don't enjoy her company very well.

I got a new purse and it's real pretty (as if you care !) Well anyway I found a nice picture of you to put inside and every time I open my purse I always look at you. Oh boy I sure do miss you!

Well, so long and please write more!

Love,
Cynthia R

To this gratifying note I replied:

Dear Cynthia,

I miss you already. Susie is coming soon to keep me company. Stephen (ugh) and Peter (ick) are always going places and playing and having all sorts of fun and all I do is be by myself. I wish Stephen would drop in a hole! He is such a brat!!! Well, I really miss you too and feel better after getting this steam out. Thanks for looking after Bootsie. I sure worry about her.

xoxoxoxoxoxoxoxoxoxoxoxoxoxoxoxoxLove,xxoxoxoxoxoxoxox
Lesley C.

Dear Lesley,

I miss you more than ever. I may die because of it! Ho Ho. I remember when it was a Saturday morning after art class and Annie, you and me were in your room and you had a picture of Susie on your bulletin board and you took it down and started hugging it and saying, "Oh, I just can't wait to see her in Boonville!" and you were kind of mad at me that day so you wanted for me to be jealous and you know what?... I was! Then you started calling me "Fatty" and said "You aughta lose some weight." Boy, then I was really mad at you! I bet you feel differently about Susie now, or do you?

Well so long and please write!

Love,

Cynthia R.

P.S. You have to write or I'll die!!!

Dear Cynthia,

I got the second letter you sent today. That day I called you "Fatty" was because you were going over to Annie's house and I wasn't invited. That's why I was mad at you and that's why I called you that dumb name ! Susie has arrived and I can tell you this - I sure wish you were here instead! Oh my goodness - we could have sooo much fun climbing in and out of windows at night etc. Susie doesn't smoke or drink or ANYTHING! That's why I miss you. And she FLIRTS with Stephen and Peter. Can you believe that? I am so disgusted. Boy I sure would like to have a good ole smoke with you in secret. Or something. Maybe a good ole beverage from the ole cupboard too.

How's the weather? Hey I'm still your best friend aren't I? You are mine of course. Your letters always bring me back to my sweet ole memories of you and me together. Of course I know you miss me and I KNOW I miss you, which I do. I'm GLAD, so there!

Well I'll write soon if you will too!

Love,

Les

← SHOES!

WIN A ROXBURY CARPET!

Does our picture intrigue you? Write us what you imagine happened. A sad story? A happy ending? Your short story (200 words more or less) may win you a Roxbury Carpet for one, two or three rooms in your home. 20 other prizes of value. Your nearest Roxbury dealer has *your* entry form. If you don't know his name, write Roxbury Carpet Company, 295 Fifth Avenue, New York 16, N.Y.

Shown: *Piroutte*, a wonderful all-wool broadloom for Roxbury's Saxonville, (Mass.) Mill.

Dear Lesley,

Please write to me and tell me what you think of this picture. It's a contest to win a Roxbury carpet. They are real pretty and I think you could win one and surprise your parents. All you have to do is describe what that woman is doing standing on the carpet and taking her shoes off. I think she came home late and doesn't want to wake up the family. The red dress is real pretty don't you think? I'll bet she was at a party. Maybe she was sneaking to it! Think about it. All you have to do is write a story and win a whole house full of carpet!

Guess what! We're taking the California Zephyr down to Disneyland. I can't wait! I wish you were with us or I was in Boonville with you. I miss you so much!

Love,
Cynthia

Dear Cynthia,

I hope your trip to Disneyland is fun. Mom says she doesn't want the carpet on our concrete floors. I thought she might not. Oh well. It is a very interesting picture anyway. I bet you are right ... that woman is up to no good and she is in BIG trouble or she wouldn't be taking her shoes off and trying to sneak upstairs like that. Do you think your mother might want the carpet?

I am enclosing a picture of those terrible bugs I told you about. They live in France. Do you remember? They have beautiful wings under those hard shells. Aren't they awful looking? They even have HORNS! I want you to keep this picture so I can have it back when I get home. O.K.?

Love,
Lesley C. xoxoxoxoxoxoxo

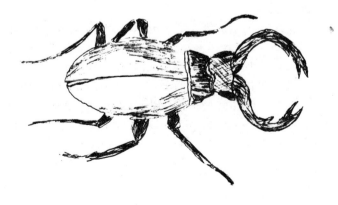

Dear Lesley,

Excuse the sloppy writing but as you know it is awfully shaky on this train. I just ate lunch and it was delicious! We had ice-cream - very chocolatey with whipped cream on top - for dessert (YUM). The train is just beautiful and I miss you very very much! This is very sincere :

I love you.
With all my heart,
Cynthia Raffel   xoxoxoxoxoxox

P.S. By the way, Les, we are going FIRST CLASS.
Ta-ta
Good-bye

Dear Cynthia Darling!

It's been sooo long! My heart has ached many a night for your sweet lips and gentle smile. How I long to hear your sweet voice and hold your lovely white paws in mine! Oh dearest! To me you are but an angel sent from the heavens above. Could I but see and hear your voice for one moment I should swoon in sheer joy. When the grass rustles and the wind hums by I can almost see you sitting in the jungle glade overhead in all your splendor. Sometimes I even try to climb a branch to reach your beautiful self. Oh! But we would take such long walks together in the moonlight and maybe stop to pet the dear sweet kangaroos. Don't give way to the dreadful chimpanzees below, Darling, pull yourself up, don't let go!

So long ole bean!

P.S. Today I swallowed a horsefly. As I was choking away in misery, mother cruelly laughed and said "Well dear, that will teach you not to leave your mouth hanging open". Naturally I let my mouth sort of drop when I'm thinking (who wouldn't?) She's always telling me to close my mouth. It was a HUGE black horsefly and it actually buzzed on the way down. There was nothing to do about it and thinking about it now makes me sick. I just thought you should know.

Howdy Pardner!

I just love reading your letters! Did you really swallow that horsefly? Wowie! It must have been a near death experience! Did you get a stomach ache or anything?

Today we went shopping and mommy practically bought the whole place out. A nice ole lady, she gave us a jar of wild blackberry jam grown only in Canada! Boy, it's delicious! Then I got you something (it was expensive of course). Boy I bet you'll really like it! Har! Har!

We went on an eight mile hike. Gosh it was swampy in places! But occasionally we would come to a big meadow and it was all green with little yellow flowers all over. But I haven't come to the best part yet! Well there were these big steep banks of snow and we would climb up to the top and slide down. Boy! Was it ever fun! You'd just go skiing down on your feet as fast as anything! SH-SH-H-H-! That is when I really wished you were here with me!

Of course I always miss you and you naturally always miss me. I sure hope you can bear Susie for three more weeks. Is she really bad? Tell me when you get home. If you ever get home! I sure wish you wouldn't be gone so long. Gosh. Right now I am beginning to miss you like ᴎᴣ⅄. (Turn that upside down).

Mommy found out that I was reading *Peyton Place* and then she saw me taking money out of Emily's piggy bank and then she got mad at me for some reason or other,

28

and she said she didn't like the way I was developing into an unclean and a not very nice girl. BUT I'm getting on good terms with her now. Disappointed? (just kidding) Well, good luck with Susie!

Love,

xoxoxoxoxoCynthia R. xoxoxoxox

Dear Cynthia,

Well today the boys (yuk) did a really disgusting thing. They are so horrible I can only tell you it is a trial to live in the next room. They both have gas - and I mean BAD - all the time, and they think it's funny. Anyway, they went into Susie's and my room every time they farted and kept our door shut the whole day and when Susie and I went up to bed we almost fainted from the odor. Could anything be worse? Susie told Mom and Dad and made a big scene about it. So I began to see the humor. She's got no brothers you understand. I mean they are just disgusting, but they can't help it.

Then I got mad at Peter later and hit him over the head with my jar of Noxema skin creme. He was pretty impressed I guess. I wish you had been there.

Love,

Lesley

P.S. You haven't forgotten that we are going up in a balloon have you? We must make it very simple. First the weather balloon, second - fish net, third - large clothes basket. (light, not heavy), fourth - very long strong rope. Would it be O.K. with you if I get the balloon (two dollars) and you get either the basket or the net? Maybe Mrs. Brand has an extra large basket you could buy for a reasonable price. When I get home we can go to the army surplus store and inquire about a net. Don't tell ANYONE about this

Oh gee, we've just GOT to do this! Don't answer questions if people ask about our little experiment. And no matter what you've GOT to find a basket!

Guess what - we may buy a paradise up here. A huge (10 acre) lake with a beaver dam and 40 acres of wildlife and forest and a house and barn. And that's not all! If we buy it you MUST come with me and spend the whole summer! Just think! Boy, you and me! Just you and me!

Well, don't get your hopes up too high. By the way we would have donkeys maybe, cows, dogs, cats, pigs, chickens, etc.

Love,
Les (forever) Snookum x to z

Y*ippee!*

Dear Les,

Boy I sure hope you get to buy the paradise you wrote about and I get to come with you! I think I'll die if we aren't together next summer!

We took our new puppy Daisy up to the mountains with us and she didn't get sick once. All she did was sleep and chew up things. She just loves it up here running all over the place. She looks so irresistible we let her sleep with us right under the covers! Mommy tells her to get off and she rolls her little eyes around and looks so sad! I'm afraid we are spoiling her.

Daddy bought some fishing rods today for us. We are going fishing tonight. He put some worms in the refrigerator and Mommy thought it was peanut butter and nearly fell over! I bought tons of chewing gum for myself.

Love,
Cynthia (S-Z)

Dear Cynthia,

I just had a brain storm while walking alone in the meadow. If we come here next year I have an idea how you can come with us!

If we raise HENS this winter and since I get $1.70 a week and you get your clothes allowance of $12.00 a month we could save up enough money so that when you and I persuade our parents to let you come we would have enough money saved up so that when we got here you and I could hike all over the country practically! Also if there isn't enough room in the car for you we could both pitch in and practically pay for a plane ticket for you!

But in order to have enough money for this we must both SAVE, SAVE, SAVE! Just get the neediest clothes we need and no candy or junk! Do you agree? We just CAN'T fail another summer! Just imagine yourself and me hiking with a pack on our back all over and sleeping out and washing in the brook and just being carefree and going ANYWHERE we wanted to. (We would have some sort of arms to protect ourselves with), and when we came to a village we would get some food.

Oh! It should be so much fun! It's just the kind of country around here where you can travel on foot and there's nobody around to stop you. Of course we wouldn't travel very far or a great distance but we would travel pretty far up in the hills and places. If you are like you are, in my opinion you will agree with me that this is the kind of life we both love!

You and me. Well, I sure wish you were here and we could do it now If only your parents would let you fly to Utica, we could meet you...and then... Anyway, write and tell me what you think of my idea, and if possibly there's any chance of you coming up. After all, the summer is still young. Please write. I love you and I really mean it too!

Love,
Les (S-Z)

Dear Les,

Daisy is growing like crazy. Boy! Also your kitty cats are all just fine. Here are some photos of them Also I'm sending this picture of Danny Kaye to you because it reminds me so much of you. It has a great resemblance don't you think so?

If you're interested I am very mad at Ruthie and I don't want to play with her anymore. She wouldn't share her Babe Ruth with me because she said it had HER name on it! She always gets something delicious in her lunchbox.

Oh Les, I can't wait until you get back. I miss you terribly as usual. Please come home.

Love,
Cynth (S-Z)

Dearest Cynthia,

Susie went home today and I don't think I've ever been so happy to see anyone leave so much! Susie was horrible. She talked all the time and just to put it in so many words she was a FLIRT, FLATTER and WINDBAG and that's the correct description of her too! My whole family has just had to admit that I should have taken you with me.

P.S. Guess what? I have a grand idea! We could buy two old balloon tired bicycles and make a tandem! And we could ride to school together on it. They go real fast. Oh boy! If you agree it will really be fun! A tandem is a bicycle built for two. You and me that is. Boy oh boy! That means that we would bicycle to and from school and on the way up and back we would stop for eats, treats, etc. What fun! Better than walking!

Please write or else!

Good ole me (X-S)

Dear Les,

Enclosed is a picture of you that I want you to auto-graph and send back right away. Also a match that you can light and think of me.

Dear S - Z,

What an awful picture you sent me to autograph of myself. Naturally I must decide not to send it back. You couldn't possibly remember me right with that ghastly thing! Soon I will send you a picture of my REAL self, heh, heh. It will look something like this:

Love,
ZORRO

P.S. You don't know how glad I am to have the photos of the kittens. If I ever did see or know a better friend than you I never knew it. Only a true-blue friend would write so much and take care of things back home for me.

P.P.S. Last night I dreamed about you - just the way you look too,. And I was so happy to see you again that I laughed in my sleep so hard that I wet my pants (a bit) I just can't wait to get home to see you, and Bootsie, and her kittens.

How do you like my idea about making the tandem? Your father and mine could maybe help a bit? All we need are two old tired bikes that won't cost very much. Wow! We'd be the envy of everybody in Palo Alto! Please write and say whether you agree or not.

I have read Booth Tarkington's three books on Penrod and *Pippi Goes Abroad.* Boy! Do we have a lot to do when

I get home again! If your father can still supply us with helium I can get the balloon. They only cost $2.00 for a 12 foot balloon! If you decide you'd like to try going up in the air with me it would be a great help if you sent $1.00.

I'm still looking for a present for you here. We must do one experiment at a time. So which do you want to do? Build the tandem or do the balloon job? I'm eager about both, but I do think we aught to do the balloon job first. We have let people think we aren't brainy enough to do it. Even if it takes all the money we have we've got to show our families that you and I have nerve and we don't fail in something we've set out to do.

Boy, let's always stick together. We have so much in common and we have a LOT OF NERVE. I think you're swell, and if you think I'm swell then there's no reason why we shouldn't be partners.

Love,
Les (S - X)

Dear Les,

I think that is a fine idea about the balloon. So I am sending $1.00 as you asked for, but please just spend it on the balloon. I can't afford to have it spent on junk.

I don't quite know about that bicycle built for two. I think it would be fun to make one though, but to go to school on it ? Well, maybe that's going a little too far.

But boy! Would I ever like to raise CHICKENS and see their eggs! We could really make some money!!!

Love,
Cynthia R.

Dear Ole Bean,

How are you? I presume fine. I miss you immensely. I'm going to see some cows today. That dog Trixie came over just now and helped sing church hymns. I gave some catnip to the neighbor's cat named Gertrude and she started to lick it and lie on it and rub it and hissed and went under the bed with it and hasn't come out since.

Guess what! Well, I just figured out what kind of present to buy you and it cost quite a bit. It's not nice to tell how much presents cost but since we are such good friends and tell each other everything it cost $5.95 plus tax!

Love,

Les

P.S. Are you boy crazy yet? I sure hope not - remember our little motto: BOYS STINK. And I mean it. Boy, I sure wouldn't like you if YOU of all people went BOY CRAZY and became a make out! Anyway, as long as we both agree that boys are just the same or pretty near slugs, we are O.K.

P.P.S. Little whispering, gossiping, nauseating, superstitious old hags at every corner!

Dear ole Pardner,

I hate boys so don't worry about that!

In case you're interested I'm not speaking to Annie anymore. Yesterday we were in the kitchen at her house and we were eating some cake and she said, "Cynthia, I think you are a PIG" Just like that. "That's not a very nice to say about a person" I said. I was really shocked! She said, "I don't care. I still think you are a PIG."

Well, I'm not going to play with her anymore.

Love,

S - Z

Dear ole pal ole Cynthia Bean,

Who cares about Annie anyway. The present I'm getting you cost $5.95!! But I think you're worth every penny of it!

Will you check once more and see if Bootsie is O.K.? I'll just die if I don't see you the minute I get home so you'll be there won't you? I sure wish you'd change your mind about being a public health nurse when you grow up. We could make real neat show business partners and it would always be you for me and me for you. Have you missed me more than you ever have before? Well, I've missed you more than ever. Soon we'll be together!!!

Well, so long closest friend, pal, partner, chum lover, buddy, neighbor, and everything else,

LOVE,

Lesley C. XOXOXOXOXOX

Dear Les,

I thought you should have this so you can carry it with you. I want you to send me one too, for my new purse.

Miss Lesley Ann Crosten is my eternal everlasting BEST FRIEND. "We shall hang together"

Signed respectfully,

CYNTHIA RAFFEL

Snookum Z

Going Up In A Balloon

With the advent of sixth grade, Cynthia and I began our dream project of GOING UP IN A BALLOON. This was the perfect escape. We sent for weather balloons of questionable vintage from an ad off the back of a Little Lulu Comic. I constructed a massive netting of decaying, frayed rope. We even acquired a large old wicker laundry basket suitable for carrying us and sundry snacks up-up and away!

Cynthia's beloved Uncle Bert, one of those rare adults who remains forever young at heart and exuberantly attentive to all outings and young people of promise, appeared to be the only grown person who believed in this project, and we felt that he would procure the necessary gases to send us aloft. Somehow.

However, on the morning before the fateful, if not fatal launching, when I test pumped up the balloons in Cynthia's living room amidst the jeering and (I suspected) *jealous* laughter of her sisters, the balloons were mysteriously full of small holes.

"You weren't really going up in that dumb thing anyway!"

"We were too!"

"Were not!"

"Uh huh!"

"Well now you sure aren't. Ha Ha."

Our project as well as our dream of skipping school forever were consequently dashed.

Oh well.

A Bicycle Built For Two

Stephen and Peter, it must be admitted, did once in a great while draw our admiration and respect. One Saturday morning I remember hearing a clattering racket outside. Down the road came Peter, stretched out on an ancient chaise lounge to which he had attached a lawn mower engine and wheels. There was a very undependable steering mechanism at his feet. He motored around the yard to the family's delight and astonishment. It was a brilliant invention, even though it crashed irreparably on the way home.

The boys then beat us at putting bike frames together to create tandems with moveable joints in the middle. They eventually hooked three bikes together and could actually bend going around corners. The best part was that Peter learned to ride the last bike facing backwards.

Cynthia and I copied their technique, constructing our own tandem using my old bike and her sister Emily's newish one, for which we never apologized and should probably do so now, and we bicycled all over on this unstable contraption until Cynthia caught her petticoat in the spokes causing us to crash. In trying to extract the petticoat her finger then got wedged for some uncomfortable minutes in the spokes.

"Yikes, Les! Wait a second...My finger is stuck!"

"Well for crying out loud it's all those stupid petti-coats! They're in the way!"

"No, don't! Just a minute for goodness sake! Don't tear the petticoats - they're Gail's and she'll kill me if she finds out I borrowed them...OUCH!"

"Hey, your finger's really wedged in there, boy oh boy... Hmm...maybe we can bend the spokes with this little stick over here..."

"Ooph! Oh my gosh, look at that!" Cynthia bent down and intently examined her finger.

"Look at what for crying out loud?"

"Look at that, just look!" She pointed to a pink spot over the middle joint of the offended finger. "See? I tell you it's *gone!*"

"Well I'll be darned. It *is* gone!"

In extricating her finger a tiresome wart of many years had been miraculously severed. No trace of it remained except for a pink spot.

6¢
U.S. POSTAGE

Closet Sleeping

Gradually Cynthia and I became so inseparable that we felt we should not be apart at night. Consequently Cynthia made a paper mache mask in my mother's art studio, which we sincerely believed looked a lot like her, even though it was formed over a watermelon and was maroon colored. It did have long black braids made from a discarded mop and the face was undeniably round. This we put on her pillow, plumping up with wadded clothing a sleeping figure under the spread.

Now she could sneak over at bedtime to tap at my window. My room had small windows which she could barely squeeze through, and there was the ever present danger of getting stuck and giggling halfway in. We laid a narrow sleeping pallet, which must have been terribly uncomfortable, on the floor of my closet.

Cynthia WAS a sport. We were both enthralled with the secret life we were living. However, it was impossible not to arrive late to school each morning after all the scurrying around pretending to be normal at both houses. We took turns hiding in the school bathroom so as not to arrive together and arouse suspicion. The teacher was in any case becoming curious and irritated with our staggered lateness. Then my father jogged into the bedroom one morning in his cheerful way and saw legs sticking out of my closet. The game was up.

We were not really in any trouble. Mother and Father smiled because we were just the goofy girls whose antics they had come to enjoy. By now our families were becoming fast friends and often got together for picnics and long walks. Our parents supported our friendship. It wasn't as though we needed to hide or sneak to be together. It was just more romantic.

U.S. POSTAGE 6¢

Muddy Conventions

Cynthia and I rarely let a day drift by idly in winter time since there was always something worth doing. If there was a heavy enough rain we prepared for a Holy Roller Convention, such as we had seen on T.V., in the lower lot of my yard. We did embellish our Conventions considerably. They began with the donning of old clothes and the selection of the perfect location - which had to have the smooth look of adobe mud without grass or rocks underneath. We would stamp on this ground until it began to loosen and sag. By continuing to work, or knead the area, we could eventually form a very deep mudhole of perhaps three feet in diameter. Then we would begin to get the "spirit" and one of us would be the preacher yelling about God and Jesus saving us from our awful sins while the other would be the poor sinner speaking in tongues and praising the Lord, dancing in the mud, anointing herself and the preacher liberally with mud until we were both completely covered from head to foot. A typical convention went like this:

First of all the preacher says reverently,
"Lord HELP YOU, Sinner Woman, PRAISE JESUS, Amen."
Then the preacher gets tough.

"OH FIE, FIE, get DOWN on your knees, Sinner Woman, and BEG FOR FORGIVENESS!"

The sinner capitulates with:

"OH YES! INDEED I AM AN AWFUL SINNER! OH HALLELUJAH, PRAISE THE LORD!"

Now the preacher sanctimoniously adds,

"AMEN, SISTER, SAY AMEN!"

The sinner, with mounting enthusiasm, cries,

"AMEN! OH JESUS! I BELIEVE I AM SAVED!"

At this point the sinner falls into the mud. The preacher, looking down upon the sinner, says,

"LET US LOOK TO THE LORD...FOR OUR SALVATION!"

The sinner now shrieks,

"YES! OH YES!"

The preacher yells back,

"HALLELUJAH, HALLELUJAH! PRAISE GOD! PRAISE HIM! OH BLESSED LITTLE LAMB JESUS SAVES! LITTLE LAMB OF GOD!!!"

The preacher now grabs a big glob of mud saying,

"SISTER! Let us be ANOINTED in the SALVATION OF THE LORD!"

To this the sinner gleefully replies,

"YES, OH YES!"

The preacher slaps mud on the sinner's head and the sinner at first squawks, then begins to speak in tongues,

" Y A B B L E . . . D A B B L E . . . D O ...BLITHER...BLAH...BLAH..."

The sinner in her mounting spirit of rapture now begins anointing the preacher's head, screeching,

"OH LORD! HAVE MERCY, OH MERCY! MERCY! HALLELUJAH! MERCY!"

Then together, screaming "MERCY! MERCY!", smeared with mud, slogging and swirling like lumps of fudge in a great tureen, both sinner and preacher burst into the realms of Nirvana, Unbounded Joy, and Blessedness.

Mother did not mind our carrying on so fervently as she was in her art studio quite oblivious to the noise, productively teaching her students, and because she was a religious skeptic who strongly believed in freedom of speech along with the pursuit of happiness and/or religion. As long as we stripped and hosed off outside when we were done with our mud baths we were allowed to indulge ourselves to our utmost satisfaction. However a good Methodist neighbor overheard the noise one day and claimed that we were actually stopping cars with the sacrilege and might cause accidents on the road. Mother, who cared about the neighbors' personal comfort, declared the show to be at an end.

We were now forced to flee to the rolling grassy hills behind the house, where we and my brother and Peter discovered that COWS have far superior mud wallows than we ever dreamed of making. The boys acquired elderly tricycles and starting at the top of a hill, we would take turns, legs straight out on either side of the tricycle, rolling at dizzying speeds down the bumpy hill to the bottom where we would fly over the edge of the wallow and land with a murky splash in the middle of the most glorious mud imaginable.

Cynthia and I, on the sly, began taking secret naked baths up in those hills, chanting the heavenly song:

"Mud, mud, GLORIOUS mud!
There's nothing quite like it for cooling the blood!
So come let us follow!
Right down to the hollow!
Where we can wallow!
In GLORIOUS MUD!"*

Hippopotamus - Written by Michael Flanders and Donald Swann from the album At the Drop of a Hat. Angel Records (#35797). 1959.

Then one day Cynthia saw a bush move with the boys hidden behind it spying on us with a cheap army surplus telescope. Being watched like that by two nerdy pubescent boys was unspeakably revolting. We could only think of them as traitors. We realized that they must hence forth be regarded strictly as *hostile forces on the loose.*

After this spying incident we returned the mud wallows to the cows.

U.S. POSTAGE 6¢

Blood Feuds and Moonlight Rambles

Our next project was crawling through drainage culverts with buckets to find native clay of a sandstone variety. This we would dig up and haul back to Mother's studio where we assiduously modelled large Peruvian women with very small heads. When they dried they were hard like cement and heavy as boulders, and if they had been thrown off the roof they would have bounced or left a crater in the earth like a small meteor. We were terrifically pleased and mother helped us to make them into desk lamps which we exhibited and used for many years.

One evening as I sat by my Peruvian Woman Lamp studying some endlessly boring detail of American History, I kept smelling licorice. Finally I located the source, to my surprise and delight. Mother had cleverly uncoiled a long rope of black licorice from the floor to my lamp as though it were the lamp cord. There it lay deliciously black and fragrant just waiting to be discovered and nibbled off, inch by inch.

There were early mornings, and moonlit nights when I slipped noiselessly into Cynthia's house, drifted stealthily up the stairs, and into her bedroom to awaken her so that we could go prowling. We would glide silently out into the night, clothed only in our long flannel nightgowns and stalk through neighbor's gardens like apparitions, feeling the exhilaration of being truly wild and free. It is wondrous to be awake in the "stolen" hours before dawn, when all the world is asleep. Our neighborhood was silent, available and refreshingly unfamiliar. The night world was not just the day world darkened. It was another world altogether.

Then early one Saturday before dawn, drifting through a neighbors garden after having seen an Appalachian blood feud on T.V., we sneakily carried all the moveable objects - portable barbecue, lawn mower, yard tools, brooms, folding chairs, salt and pepper shakers, and one spare tire from two carports that were under a small duplex and switched everything, imagining that this would begin a dramatic confrontation between the two households. We stole nothing but we did take the risk of being caught in our conspiracy. For several days we meandered by hoping to witness some kind of feud, but we never heard anything, to our actual relief.

Mystery of the Sanitary Napkins

What's to be done when one stumbles upon a whole box of unused Kotex on the side of the road on an otherwise ordinary Saturday morning? Cynthia naturally called me immediately.

"Les! I found something BIG on my way home! No one else knows about it and I've hidden it *under my bed!*"

"Well, what is it?" I asked impatiently.

"I can't SAY over the phone", she whispered hoarsely, "It's a SECRET and I only want YOU to see it!"

"I'll be there right away!" I exclaimed, grabbing an uncooked hotdog out of the refrigerator, a handful of walnuts from the cupboard, three slices of Profile bread from the drawer and an orange on my way out.

I trotted over to Cynthia's house, munching excitedly, to examine her secret. Kotex did not just sit around our homes - it fell into the category of "discrete female hygiene" and although I had seen a movie at school that made no sense to me at all - I was actually more interested in eating my fudgesicle which was the reward for attending the movie - I just never imagined any of this particular subject matter involved me. Cynthia had a slightly better idea of the function of these peculiar feminine napkins because she had older sisters. But neither of us really knew what to do with them. Basically it all boiled down to the fact that we had a treasure and we would somehow make use of it - invent, if need be - a value for it.

We therefore tried to fit the napkins on, more or less, one at a time, and then in order to really experience them, we peed a little bit on each one. Then we hid them in the closet until dark. And then, for some strange reason, or lack of reason, we just tossed them out of her upstairs window and went to bed.

Cynthia's window faced the front yard and the street, and her parents bedroom was right next to hers. The following morning we remembered that we had tossed out the Kotex.

"Gosh, Les! Look what we've done!" Cynthia peered sleepily out the window.

We scurried downstairs and out to collect the debris terrified lest someone, especially her mother awaken and stroll outside to water the flowers. Each napkin had fluttered down and landed on the fronds of a large palm tree that grew next to her window. The tree was bedecked with waving Kotex napkins as though it were promoting a tacky sales convention. We had to fetch a rickety ladder very quietly and pry the napkins off their palm fronds with a long stick. The Angel of Mercy was with us that morning because miraculously we did not get caught.

Rituals

There are certain rituals that comprise the inner fabric of deep, girlhood friendship. Up in the hills behind our houses we created secret names for each other, a formal anthem, as well as solemn marching and saluting to go with the anthem. Over time there evolved a mysterious and rather poisonous "elixir" consisting of various alcoholic beverages snatched from our father's forbidden stock, fruits, twigs, pepper, and dried items which when finally mixed together were too suspiciously vaporous and evil looking for either of us to dare swallow. However we considered this a potion of magical power and hid it beneath Cynthia's kitchen stairs, where it possibly remains to this day. From time to time we added more curious ingredients to it. Just knowing it was there gave us a powerful feeling.

There was always the white picket fence, our secret meeting place that was never mentioned aloud by name for fear of discovery, and most importantly, we had a certain elbow nudge which could be used when we needed to make contact, to confirm our mutual delight or disgust over anything or anybody, including ourselves. The nudge was generally enough to cause us to snuffle, twitch or giggle at inopportune moments amongst company. Our understanding and sympathy at this moment was complete enough to make us feel like a small nation.

At Christmas time it was a tradition for the faculty children to be the choir at the campus church for the Christmas Eve service. About two weeks before Christmas we were dutifully assembled in the church basement by the choir director and lined up two by two according to our vocal range and physical size. In the early years, because I was a full head taller than Cynthia, I hunched down while she stood on tiptoes so that we appeared of similar height and were allowed to march together down the isle of the church in our flowing red choir robes.

It was an emotional time, especially for the choir director, because few of us could sing well. The director was both sensitive and temperamental, balding with a fringe of scraggily grey hair, and in these demanding sessions he began calmly enough, speaking to us endearingly through his nose, enunciating every vowel and consonant with the utmost care.

"Oh, you darling children, come and let us sing together!"

He soon became tearful and impatient with our efforts.

"OPEN YOUR MOUTHS! How else do you expect SOUND to come forth??? Breathe deeply now...in, out...in, out...SING FROM YOUR HEARTS, children, FEEL THE BEAUTY of these words!"

Then he would begin again with "*Lo, How a Rose Ere Blooming,*" which was about as meaningless as our daily school song about "purple mountains' majesties above the fruited plains".

The poor man wheedled with us, hurt that we were not in tune, furious that we whispered, poked each other, or twitched. He became outraged that we had weak, uneven voices. It was clearly a dreadful experience for him. He was used to a talented and mature choir. The nearer the performance time, the more exasperated and hysterical he became, and the more he thundered, wept, and tore his hair.

On Christmas Eve he would desperately go off looking for the minister, with whom he would confer. The minister would then come and pray over us, suggesting that we might for that BRIEFEST of concerts, sing in tune and prettily together.

The whole experience was initially alarming. It did not seem like fun and I therefore wondered why we were doing it. But over the years it became important to the meaning of Christmas to be part of the midnight service, and I do believe we actually sounded, on Christmas Eve, rather celestial. At the stroke of midnight, when the Baby Jesus was officially born, the whole congregation stood up and sang "Joy to the World." Cynthia and I then solemnly turned to each other and shook hands as we chanted the final verse to our anthem:

"We will go through all the wars together
Hang, Hang, Hang together!
For we are the Snookums!
A rum te tee tum!"

We had an unspoken promise not to grow up into something other than what we were. I perceived there to be a threat of one kind or another to our sanity lurking in the air but as yet I had not identified the actual extent of the menace. We both wore undershirts, stalked one another with imaginary sixguns, and danced in a circle holding hands and singing until we collapsed in our laughter. We were devoted, we were safe with each other, and that was life in blessed wholeness. We were then eleven years old.

U.S. POSTAGE   6¢

Junior High School

The following year we were collectively bussed to the junior high school across town to begin the seventh grade. Suddenly we, a white group of twenty faculty children, the majority of whom had been sheltered together since kindergarten, were diffused into a mass of two hundred other seventh graders from upper white collar, lower blue collar, Black, Mexican, and Chinese neighborhoods. Cynthia and I were separated, to meet only between classes and at lunch time. At once we became numbers rather than individuals.

I hated the forced confinement, the teachers, the cement underfoot, and everything else about the school. Cynthia and I were a full year younger than the average seventh grader. Socially we were "out of it " as were most of the other faculty kids. We still wore undershirts, while many of the other girls were clearly young women. They were dating, going steady, necking on the bus, wearing nylons and massive petticoats, lipstick and eye shadow on the sly, and even bras. I felt like a heffalump.

Life was no longer sensible as it had been in elementary school. Bussing to junior high school, a flat roofed series of flesh colored sprawling barracks with small windows like a factory and low ceiling corridors in between was like commuting to a military base for the unwanted five days a week. I could not understand why parents who supposedly loved their children would intentionally bus them to a penal institute.

Stephen sprouted whiskers and grew enormous feet. He croaked like a frog and purchased a jock strap. The school chairs hurt my tailbone and my breasts got sore. The desks didn't fit. My face puffed up and erupted. It seemed like everyone was in the midst of uncontrollable stormy, giddy, or gloomy mood swings. Girls wore mountains of stiff petticoats that billowed over the chairs fastened to the desks, and pointy shoes that cramped and crippled the toes. Everything fashionable to wear was uncomfortable and made you sweat.

What helped me through those terradactylian years was a large camel hair overcoat with cargo pockets, which I donned as a solution to what I assumed was my unique problem of feeling repulsively abnormal no matter what I wore. I kept everything in my pockets and did not carry a purse. During class changes I purchased bags of stale popcorn from a machine in the corridor and munched vigorously when in doubt, which was most of the time. At lunch I bought corn nuts and a fudgesicle to complement the chipped beef or bologna sandwich brought from home. The snack shop sold sloppy joes made of gristle in a greasy orange sauce and the cafeteria tiredly provided the usual canned spaghetti with lime jello dessert. The bathrooms were always smokey from girls sneaking cigarettes in the cubicles and smoking illegally, while the toilets were often clogged from either someone's deep feelings of resentment or from the improper flushing of Kotex and/or text books. Once someone even blew up the toilets with cherry bombs. Junior high school was a miserable and insane place to spend a pretty day.

Home was my sanctuary. I never could bear to partici-
pate in extra curricular activities. I went to school under
protest even though I did feel obliged to learn my lessons
once I got there. Cynthia and I had no classes together
except for the required Home Economics. We therefore
put a lot of extra energy into having fun in that class. The
first part of the year it was a cooking class, and we learned
how to make party ice-cream with whipped cream and
canned fruit cocktail; we also made peanut brittle and
mock apple pie with ritz crackers which was beyond
awful.

Since we were partners in our "kitchen," we ate nearly
half of our ingredients before anything got cooked. We
had an uproarious time and got a poor grade.

The second half of the year was spent on sewing and
since the chairs had wheels on the bottoms we did spinning
tricks and had chair chases and misbehaved to the point
that the teacher called my mother to complain about my
attitude. She chose to personally undo and remake my
sewing project as an example for the class because I had
done such a bad job, and it was with spiteful pleasure that
I got a poor grade in sewing class - even though at home
I often sewed things for fun. I felt belittled to be forced to
take those classes that made us into conventional well
behaved young women. I came out of sewing class with a
drab brown cotton flare skirt that I could not bear to wear.

Sitting On Rocks

To crown the debacle of seventh grade I began to bleed one Saturday. It was a hot and dusty afternoon, squinty bright outside. I had a vague irritability, an inability to focus on anything in particular. There was a stirring inside me that was not pleasant. I supposed it to be gas, possibly from eating green plums. Then I began to bleed.

Buried in the bottom drawer of my mind was a recollection of the significance of this. I had over the past year noticed other unfortunate girls at school excuse themselves from gym class, and I had noticed that some girls smelled heavy, and were indrawn and preoccupied with themselves. I thought of them sadly as victims of an alien disease. Now I felt dark and broody myself, and rather sick. It was an unsafe and weak condition. I did not know what to do. I did not choose this to happen.

Mother found me crying in my room, and took me on her lap and rocked me. I sobbed broken-heartedly and felt safer rocking on her lap. Being held was extremely unusual at my age and gave me an enormous sense of comfort. But it was all too brief, and after a few minutes

Mother adjusted herself, stood me up and got briskly to business. She rummaged in a drawer, handed me a napkin and showed me how to put a sanitary belt on with the napkin securely fastened to it between my legs. Reluctantly, I felt that I was being separated from her comfort, separated from my old self- I had been thrust into a new and negative state of being. I was, after all, to become a woman. I, who had been clear and fleet footed as the wind, who did not concern myself with woman stuff, was suddenly bloated, leaky, and diapered. If only I could have stayed forever curled on her lap, or run away with the wind!

By Sunday I felt really awful. The pain that I supposed to be gas was obviously cramps from what was happening, and I hurt enough to lie on my bed most of the day. Mother was busy elsewhere in the house packing suitcases, vacuuming and storing items in preparation for our upcoming summer trip. No one paid me much attention which may have been out of awkwardness or respect, but served to heighten my miserable uniqueness. All night I worried for fear of messing my nightgown and the sheets. I tried to just lie flat on my back and not move and waited for daybreak.

When Monday morning came I heard a quail calling her chicks and felt distinctly lighter in spirit, like a brand new butterfly, a little weak and damp. I thought I might survive. I washed very carefully and sensed a familiar twinge of expectant pleasure at the thought of seeing Cynthia. She would help me decide what to take on my trip. The bleeding seemed to have subsided and my appetite was fully restored. It was with grateful relief that I saw her sauntering up the drive with a "Hey ole bean!" She looked absolutely normal, as did the sky. We spent the day packing, chatting, promising to write and wishing we were not to be separated for the summer. Secretly I was so relieved to be alive, in a familiar place, to be still recognizable to my best friend, that I could have reverently kissed a lima bean.

On Tuesday my mother, brother, and I boarded a train to visit our relatives in Gallup, New Mexico, on the way to Boonville. The train ride was exceedingly hot, stifling, and jerky. Within a few hours I began to menstruate - this time heavily - with one napkin tucked in my bag. Too ashamed to mention the problem to my mother, horrified that I was again bleeding, I went to the rattling stainless steel bathroom cubicle every half hour to check for stains and to pull out the used cotton and restuff the napkin netting with fresh toilet paper. This netting I continued to restuff and use for the next two weeks. Although I was sure there was something wrong with me I was unable to ask for help. A secret and shameful event was occurring - my fun-loving, nimble body was betraying me in the cruellest way. I was to be imprisoned, squeeze-legged onto benches next to bathrooms wherever we went, to be severed suddenly from childhood and the children who laughed and played with abandon outside, to be crammed into an invisible cage. Like the heretics in the middle ages that were hung in cages outside castle walls, I was to live my days in a despairing temple of isolation in which I was out of control and robbed of my dignity.

When we arrived in Gallup the temperature was 112 degrees, yet I was afraid to go swimming with the other children for fear of being "exposed". I could imagine floating out into the deep water, much like a cow slowly crossing the Amazon River, leaving a trail of tell tale pink streaks behind her as the piranhas attacked her underbelly. I could hardly walk and held my breath for fear of rupturing completely. My situation was unspeakable. I imagined everyone suspected something was mortally wrong with me - how could they not - but no one spoke of it, *probably because it was so terrible.*

Cunningly I drew my cousins and brother into card games so that they would not go outside to play - so that I would not be left out and could be close to the bathroom, my private torture chamber. We played interminable games of Samba in their cool adobe house. Every few minutes I held my breath and crept into the bathroom to check and restuff the now disintegrating netting. Even the smallest movement caused a dark and hot gushing. I figured I was probably bleeding to death.

When the bleeding finally stopped, it stopped for a whole year. I put it from my mind as though it had been a three week nightmare from which I awoke. In my shame I never spoke about it to anyone, not even to Cynthia.

Dance Lessons

It was in the winter of the eighth grade that our parents got together and decided to make Cynthia and me into ladies, and my brother and our next door neighbor Hank into gentlemen. Once a week we were told to put on our dancing shoes and pretty dresses, to get clean and fragrant in anticipation of pleasing our dance partners, who were, unfortunately, my brother and Hank.

As we were driven to our Arthur Murray Dance Class we tumbled about in the back seat pushing and shoving, snickering and poking until we arrived wrinkled and disheveled, the boys' ties askew, at the front door where we were instructed to stand politely and ring the bell. We were then formally greeted and lined up with our partners who occasionally forgot to zip up their flies and were now discreetly nudged to do so. We straightened our sashes, the boys retied their ties properly, we pulled up our white socks, and went into the ballroom. There we were instructed in the Cha cha cha, the Tango, and the Waltz, how not to appear too eager, how to step to the beat lightly and not on our partners' toes, and how to behave with sophisticated decorum at all times. We found ourselves exaggerating with goodwill and merriment all that we were taught. It was, to be sure, goofy and lots of fun.

The dance instructors were Fred Astaire/Ginger Rogers

look alikes. They were stunning and gracious to each other and to us. The boys, who mostly had not yet gotten their growth spurts were a full head shorter than many of the girls. As well, a general level of awkwardness and hostility pervaded the ballroom. The boys learned to say, "May I have the honor of this dance?" which actually meant, "Get up here and dance, you creep!" This was to be followed by our acquiescent reply, "By all means, it would be my pleasure!", which truthfully meant, "If I have to, toad."

Following our dance class, we often blew off steam by having a neighborhood rotten fruit fight. This was a form of guerrilla warfare in which the boys and girls were separate enemy camps. We attempted to hunt down and ambush one another. An attack was screamingly exciting with rotten persimmons flying through the air frequently on target. Unfortunately Cynthia was one afternoon ambushed at her front door, just as she came out of it unsuspectingly, and her father was watching. She received a persimmon in the eye, which made her face orange like a pumpkin and her eye black and blue. Her father sternly reprimanded the boys, calling them "young hooligans!", a term we happily added to our ever growing descriptive vocabulary for them.

U.S. POSTAGE 8¢

The First Kiss

Several Saturday nights we put our dance lessons to the test by having candle lit parties with little 45 records at one of our houses. Parents were only to be discreetly present, and absolutely invisible as we danced to a few of our favorite popular tunes again and again. My brother was in love with Garda, the closest neighbor girl. I adored a neighbor boy named Greg, who had pink cheeks and was the teacher's pet, and Cynthia was partnered up with old Hank, a bit hefty but funny and as good natured as she. One fateful evening as we were dancing to the slowest possible music, doing what we fondly called the "bunny hug" in which you just hug your partner a lot and move as little as possible, Greg kissed me on the lips. This was something that had never occurred. I had seen my brother and Garda doing it, I had certainly witnessed it in movies, and I imagined that it would be an ultimately romantic move, but I had never DONE it. I was unprepared. And I'm sorry to say it was disgusting.

That night as Cynthia and I lay in her double bed discussing the dance, I confessed to her what had happened.

"He kissed me, Cynthia," I said.

"He what?"

"He kissed me ON THE LIPS," I replied more meaningfully.

Cynthia sat upright in bed. She turned and peered down at me.

"My gosh Les! Did he really? On the LIPS??? Well, ...What was it like?....Oh my gosh, Les!"

She begged to know, so I paused for a moment, in honest reflection, and then said,

"It was horrible. Slimy. It was like two *night crawlers* stuck onto my mouth."

The recollection made me shiver. Then, as an afterthought,

"He also said I was built like a battleship."

"WOWIE!" Cynthia exclaimed.

I felt rather pleased with this compliment even though I bore no resemblance whatsoever to a battleship. Greg probably had heard his older brother use this phrase and he very possibly didn't know what it meant either.

Mercifully, our dance classes as well as our Saturday night parties came to an end around the same time, and I was not kissed again for several years, nor was Cynthia, nor was I truly smitten again for many years. Charming Greg found if not greener, more seductive pastures with more popular girls, and both Garda and Hank moved away.

Science and The Old Chevy

That same eighth grade year Cynthia and I were required to take a science class. We decided to do the classic twenty-one day gestation of the chicken experiment using her father's lab and incubator as the site for this uninspired educational waste. Every day we traipsed over to his lab after school and took one egg, opened it and examined it, then candled and turned the others. The experiment did not reach completion because the eggs began to rot after a time. We had in any case lost interest and become obsessively distracted. We were going to his lab for an entirely different experiment.

Cynthia's father drove a 1949 Chevy convertible coupe and he usually had the canvas top folded down. That car was always innocently parked along the curb below his lab. Cynthia and I would take turns wearing her father's long overcoat and hat, and our new game would begin about two blocks away from the parked car. The scenario for this gruesome escapade was always the same:

A woman, perhaps Cynthia, would be casually minding her own business, walking to the car when she would sense that someone was possibly following her. Sure enough, someone, possibly Lesley, was lurking in a long overcoat and hat far behind. The woman increased her pace a bit, turning now and then to see if the overcoated figure was still there. There could be no doubt about it. She would now hasten along more quickly, but when she looked back again the overcoated figure was definitely gaining on her, so she would at last not be able to bear it casually any longer. She would break into a run, finally reaching the car, which was wide open.

The point was to get the canvas up, and the windows zipped, and the doors locked quickly while there was time. Panic was now inevitable. Her fingers became clumsy and she fumbled and fussed, unable to pull the zippers up. She barely managed to close the side windows and lock the doors, and then heaved herself around to zip up the back window. Aak ! At this precise moment the overcoated figure arrived at the back end of the car and with a leap, scrabble, lunge and vicious growl, tumbled through the back window.

She screamed bloody murder. Naturally. Who wouldn't? This was the scariest game we ever played. Our hearts nearly stopped from the terror. We took turns playing the roles and repeated this game for several days while the eggs rotted in the lab, and then one day Cynthia's father came storming out to the parking lot and told us to stop our screaming immediately. People working at the lab were annoyed and it sounded like someone was being murdered. He was exasperated, and probably disgusted with the obviously rotting eggs in the lab. We were very sorry and apologized. It WAS embarrassing. However, we were so obsessed by this game that we then tried to play it without screaming, but it was impossible. Such a frightful game broke straight through fantasy and caused our screams to be real, and blood curdling.

Clothing Allowances

Around this time, my parents put both my brother and me on clothing allowances so that we could begin to shop for ourselves and learn to manage our living expenses. The concept was peculiar. We didn't really need anything because our parents carefully provided all of our actual necessities. But other parents were doing this, and of course we were ecstatic to suddenly, once a month, receive a lump sum of cash.

After collecting the money, Cynthia, already a seasoned clothing allowance shopper, and I immediately bicycled to the shopping center, three miles distant, where we strolled excitedly through the shops. That first month, after considerable thought, I purchased three records, "South Pacific" which I could count on my father to swoon over because he was an incurable romantic, a cool jazzy recording featuring the theme song for a television detective series for me and Cynthia, and a record of Swiss Alpine Horns calling to one another across mountain tops, which I knew would make my mother weak kneed because it touched some mystical part of her soul.

I also purchased bags of chunky carob chocolate,

convinced that it was not really bad for me and that it would not mar my complexion because it was purchased from the House of Nutrition. The man who ran the store looked seriously anemic. He had a yellowish, spotty complexion along with a runny nose, and he talked incessantly in a whining Swedish accent about colon flushes, desiccated liver, Brewers yeast, and case histories of nearly dead people. I became convinced that any candy item coming from this store was a health food. Of course the store was packed with "organic" candy, which may well have accounted for his spotty complexion. I can certainly say that my own complexion never seemed to benefit from these organic candy binges.

When I returned home, gorged on the healthiest of chocolates, I proudly played the records for my parents and they seemed very pleased. It is true that I had not purchased any clothing but mother and father appeared contented that I had broadened my musical horizons. Father swooned on the sofa to the songs of the Pacific, I slinked to the beat of 77 Sunset Strip, and Mother listened deeply to the strains of the Alpine Horns, with a faraway look in her eye.

The very next month Cynthia and I bicycled back to the shopping center. This time I determined to buy an item of clothing. At the Emporium we spied a rack of imported creme colored glossy goat skin jackets that looked not only fashionable but practical. Best of all, the jacket cost exactly my month's allowance which was twenty dollars. I wore this coat rain or shine with great pride. In reality it was oddly freezing to wear even on a warm day. It could have kept ice-cream hard. I don't know why unless it was the glossy finish which resembled a kitchen appliance, or perhaps it was the lining, also suspiciously glossy. Naturally I never admitted to anyone that it was uncomfortable.

I was certain that I was spending my money wisely, in contrast to my brother, who had by now supplemented his wardrobe with a pair of shiny very pointed black patent leather Italian shoes and peg legged pants and short sleeved shirts with the sleeves rolled up, and who was, I thought, clearly on a downhill path, probably into the bushes, with any number of willing young women. I frowned on him and his budding sexuality. It was so exceedingly obvious! I was prudish and self-righteous, careful to secure my parents' approval and admiration for the wisdom of my choices. I could not tolerate disapproval. It would have shattered me. I curried favor, courted my parents with a contrived sagacity and goodness. I worked hard to be taken seriously, believing that I could, through hard work and sensibleness, earn my way out of school or perhaps even be excused from it for good behavior and maturity beyond my years.

Cynthia was an average, well-behaved student, certainly more cheerful than most. Her teachers liked her. I was neither a great student, nor a poor student. But I was reasonably conscientious. I daydreamed a lot, and dreamed fantastic adventures at night. Like Zorro, I leapt off roof tops onto my waiting horse, won righteous fights with a bull whip, or floated nakedly through rainbow trees in the garden of Eden where pink frogs lived under pale green cobble stones. My imagination lived in a realm completely untouched by school. And it was my imagination and Cynthia's friendship that kept me alive through the dark ages of public junior high school.

At night I would sit at my desk until late modelling elves and fairies and whole miniature villages of fanciful characters - Kings with golden earhorns, mermaids, insects, fishing villages, fairies astride dragon flies, owls and other wild animals. These creations I would sit on my parents' bed stand as an offering. They seemed pleased. When I was busily sculpting some piece, mother respected my privacy and my need not to be disturbed. Unfortunately my artwork bore no relation to school whatsoever and school ate up the greater part of each day.

Strawberry Shortcake and Catfood

Mother and father gave many parties throughout the year in honor of various entertainers who performed at the university. Cynthia and I were thirteen when we contracted with my mother, for a very reasonable sum, to help out in the kitchen during these parties. We made, served, and cleaned up hors d'oeuvres and drinks. Once in a while we served dinner. We looked forward to these events mostly because the food was fantastic and we had free rein in the kitchen. We wore good dresses covered by aprons that mother had personally sewed on one of her periodic sewing sprees. One of our favorite duties was to make exotic and very artistic little taste treats to serve the guests. Of course we sampled everything that we served, including the drinks, and although we never got the staggers, we generally got tipsy. The fruitier and more complicated drinks naturally took our fancy. Taking turns with the trays, we careened through the house, replenishing people's cocktails and handing out small sandwiches, olives, nuts, grilled dainties and canapes.

The guests milled around. Perfumes intermingled with cigar smoke and cologne, evening gowns rustled and an animated din filled the air. Some ladies were eager to speak to us. Since most were colleagues of my father or neighbors who had known us since we were children, they were fascinated to watch us growing into young women. We were in that tantalizing stage of being untouchable as children, yet we were at the beginning of female transformation. Adults looked us up and down slowly, which ordinarily is quite rude, but which is apparently acceptable if one is looking at a child who is growing into a woman.

One woman never tired of exclaiming, "My, how you've grown! Why, you are becoming a beautiful young lady *after all!*" This always seemed to surprise everyone. What was excruciating was the next unfortunate line. "Come over here and let me look at you!" Drawing another nearby and uninterested guest over she would say conspiratorially, "Will you just look at her! Isn't she just the image of her mother! (or father!) How old are you now?" After this set of predictable, boring and slyly hostile remarks my tormentress would get too close and I would find myself backing into someone behind me. I could not stand being told that I was the image of either my mother or father. They were very handsome individuals so it was not an unfavorable remark in that sense, but the effort to be a unique entity is great and often agonizing at the age of thirteen.

As the evenings wore on, there were one or two men who paid us special attention. They glowingly slathered us with compliments and made remarks regarding our blossoming womanhood. We blushed and carried these comments back to the safety of the kitchen along with the dirty dishes, where we repeated them to one another, pondered or snickered over them. There was one professor who sometimes managed to catch us just outside the kitchen door and grab us for an emotional hug, pressing his front against us. We thought this repulsive, slithering out from his grasp immediately. We knew this was his predictable alcoholic behavior. We also knew him otherwise to be a kindly and talented musician.

When strawberry season came along in late spring, my parents gave a huge annual strawberry shortcake party. As the flats of strawberries arrived Cynthia and I gorged ourselves in the kitchen on homemade shortcake, strawberries with sugar and whipped cream. Then we got busy making up the guest plates. If someone was insensitive enough to abandon a plate with one bite taken out of the shortcake, we carefully whisked it back to the kitchen, patched it up good as new, plopped a dollop of whipped cream on top and took it right back out again on the serving tray. We could not imagine wasting strawberries or whipped cream. By the end of the party as we cleaned up the kitchen, we polished off our fifth or sixth plate of strawberry shortcake.

One evening, as my parents gave an elegant party in honor of an out-of-town celebrity, we ran out of expensive paté. We pondered the crisis, loath to interrupt my mother who was circulating cheerfully among her guests. Thoughtfully I went to the cupboard and brought out several cans of Puss'n Boots cat food.

"What do you think, Cynthia?

"Gosh, Les, do you think we should?"

"Well, it looks a lot like the paté, don't you think?"

I opened a can and sniffed it." Perhaps we should taste it," I suggested, handing it to her.

Cynthia firmly shook her head. "No, I don't think so."

"Well, it smells fine anyway. I suppose we'll *just have to use it.*"

Cynthia agreed that this was a reasonable solution to a delicate problem. We mashed it with cream cheese, put slices of olives, pimentos and sprigs of parsley on top of delicate crackers, arranged them gracefully on trays, sipped our wine, and sashayed out to try them on our distinguished guests.

The dainties were a hit. We received many compliments on our canapes and although no one asked for the recipe of these delectable snacks, people ate them all greedily. Clearly they relished the Puss 'n Boots, and we most generously offered the rest of it. Following this success, I personally sampled my cat's canned mackerel, which I found excellent, and the dry kibble, which I found no worse than grapenuts. However, mother knowingly said none of it was fit for human consumption and we should, in no instance, *serve* it to guests or for that matter, eat it ourselves.

Goodnight Dreams

When I went to bed at night after these parties I often had, along with mild gastric distress, a recurring dream. It was of me standing at the front door in my apron, saying goodnight to all the guests who waited in a long line to leave. I was very tired and anxious to say goodnight, and I couldn't wait for the last person to step through the door. As the last person walked away I sighed and turned back to the living room. Lo! All the guests were reassembling behind me, waiting to say goodnight again. Once more I would try to be polite, although my patience was flagging and my fatigue was unbearable, and this trick would keep happening. Somehow they kept getting back into the living room no matter how many times I showed them to the door.

This dream may have been caused by the exotic variety and quantity of foods I ingested at these parties. Why I remained slim is a mystery. In any case the dream was cruel and exhausting. My brain was caught and stuck somehow in the jumbled transition between day time and dream time and could not figure out how to free itself.

Eventually I learned to change channels - to transport myself to the "green room" in my mind. I floated to our summer home in Upstate New York and as I lay in bed I heard the whippoorwill calling its lonely song from the roof top; I snuggled down under mother's old black and white checked wool blanket, ran my fingers along the satin trim, and listened to the dark close silence of the forest that surrounded our house.

A Place Of Our Own

In the summer of my thirteenth year, my parents were finally able to purchase a fifty acre homestead five miles outside the village. The homestead was surrounded by forest land, had a ten acre pond that was once a fish hatchery, with a creek flowing into it and a large cement dam at the other end. There was a two story farmhouse in poor repair, with long glassed-in porches on two sides, a huge barn that was falling down, a pump house and a garage. It was our dream come true.

All through the school year we waited anxiously to return to our new summer home. We wrote frequent letters to our Boonville friends who seemed as excited as we over the purchase. It was even determined that Cynthia would at last be allowed to come to Boonville too, which made the count down of days until school was over more gratifying than ever before. I had a calendar by my bedside and woke up an extra hour before getting up so that I could cross off the remaining days before departure and still have time to day dream of the glorious summer ahead.

When we packed the car and drove off we were six people plus the German shepherd dog wedged into our 1950 emerald green Buick sedan. We had a rack on top carrying clothing, sleeping bags, miscellaneous picnic gear, fishing poles; a water bag was suspended over the radiator and we had an American flag waving from the antenna. We got as far as Bakersfield which was only four hours away before the valves were sticking so loudly that we feared an explosion and had to stop. The temperature was over one hundred degrees and we as well as the car were experiencing a meltdown. While the car was being repaired the first of many times, we stayed at a motel with a small swimming pool and Peter entertained us with belly flops off the diving board. No mere car breakdown could extinguish our excitement.

The long trip across the country was one of many car breakdowns, high anxiety, tears, laughter, humid heat, congestion, claustrophobia, and wild anticipation. I prayed much of the way across that we would make it, and while the engine rested from overheating in Nebraska, I made a pact with God that if we made it safely across I would read the Bible as soon as we got to Boonville. Because we did arrive safely I actually picked up and read the Bible - being good as my word - but must admit to retaining very little information or wisdom because I was so eager to get on to the pressing matters of summer living.

The Arrival

Our arrival at Jessie and John's house in Boonville was the most exciting moment of my life. I had told them so much about Cynthia over the years, and I had told her so much about Boonville that this meeting of Jessie and John and Cynthia IN Boonville was, from my point of view, one of those rare moments of perfection in life. What more can you ask, at thirteen, than to live with your eternal best friend in paradise for a whole summer?

It was a tradition to stay the first night with Jessie and John. Then the following morning we would all go together to our summer camp. But this enchanted summer we wanted to go straight to our own homestead, so after first spilling out of the car to greet Jess and John, at which time our dog raced excitedly upstairs and peed on their wallpaper, we all drove the five miles out of town and turned off onto our own private road through the woods.

Cynthia and I chose to walk in. The path was sandy with a sweet smelling cover of pine needles, ferns and wintergreen with the occasional lady slipper tucked beneath gnarled scotch pines. Here and there were elegant spreading white pines and sugar maples and paper white birch trees with shimmering leaves. We took off our shoes and slowly walked around the bend, then we dropped into the clearing where we saw the great collapsing barn, the garage, and further up the hill on a knoll overlooking the pond sat the farmhouse.

We ran barefoot up to the house where we were completely taken by surprise. Our friends, over the cold winter months, had furnished, bit by bit, the entire house, from carpeting, beds, sofas, chairs, tables, to linens, blankets, towels, kitchen utensils, and even curtains. The only thing missing was ourselves. We all sat down and just wanted to cry because it was overwhelming.

Perhaps because of this the property became a gathering place for friends. Everyone felt a sense of belonging.

Everyone had some old familiar thing in use at our camp. Our gatherings spanned three generations - Jessie's parents and their friends, Jess and John and all those friends who were my parent's age, and Cynthia, Peter, Stephen and me as well as the many young people whom we brought home from the village. Summertime was a gathering time for many loving people who helped us create a wonderful extended family.

Settling In

Clothing made sense in the summertime. We kept a big dresser full of miscellaneous old clothes - socks, shirts, pants, swim suits - that anyone might rummage through and try on.

There was an outfit for all those who came to stay, providing they were not fussy about the fit or style. Cynthia and I loved wearing old soft flannel shirts and oversize pants with rolled up cuffs. There were favorite rags to rediscover each year. They contained within their faded colors, patterns, and patches memories of other summers, of special people who had come to visit and had worn them. And people brought their old clothes and left them for the next visit. Cynthia and I brought our blue one piece snap up gymsuits as our preferred all purpose garment. We wore these most of the time that first summer, even swimming in them. There were shelves of worn out shoes, boots, sandals, but we spent most of the time at home barefoot.

Days followed a schedule at camp because there was so much work to be done. Mornings, we had a rowdy farm breakfast. We all sat down together in the breakfast alcove and chatted over bacon, eggs, toast, homemade strawberry jam, melon, and milk. The local radio station's news and weather chirruped cheerfully in the background. One of us occasionally yelled that the toast was on fire because the toaster didn't pop up. Following breakfast we trudged down the hill to work on one of the large projects. The first was tearing down and burning the collapsed barn.

In the lower floor of the barn we found a doctor's buggy in fair condition which we pulled up and down the road with two people substituting as horses. We also found a huge wooden sleigh and a clumsy balloon tire bicycle with rusty metal seat and only the metal rims left on the wheels. Peter bicycled around a lot on this - mostly down bumpy hills. We all experienced sore crotches from bouncing over rocks with neither a seat pad nor rubber tires. Somehow we never bothered to put new tires on it.

After we had torn down, carried away and burned the mountain of debris that was the old barn, we began to carry away piles of rusty garbage from the woods. We planted new trees and thinned old ones, painted the house trim inside and out and put in a small beach area next to the pond. We all worked hard together and were very dirty and tired by the time mother called us to lunch. We ate a big, noisy lunch of many assorted items mother found to put on the table. Not everything was edible or even identifiable but mother unflinchingly made every effort to recycle leftovers at lunch time. After this we either scattered to do our own projects or went off to visit a favorite swimming hole on the Moose River or to follow the railroad trestle and then a meandering path through a cow pasture to the hidden Dry Sugar Falls. There we basked in the sun and played in the waters until late afternoon when it was the hour to return home for dinner and croquet games.

Summer Projects

Cynthia and I built both a tree house and a raft that first summer. The tree house was located down in the woods near the dam and was made of salvaged lumber and tin roofing from the barn. It was very basic, just a walled-in tin roofed platform in between three scotch pines. Mother called it an eyesore. We fitted it out with comforters, pillows and cans of fruit cocktail and Hostess cupcakes and slept in it when we were tired of family. It was spooky at night in the woods because of all the wild sounds - snuffling woodchucks, raccoons, skunks, red fox and black bear, owls and the dreadful screams of dying rabbits. The wild noises were enough to make a fitful and sleepless night, but then our independence was worth a great amount of suffering.

For the raft we sawed our own small dead pine tree down, and used old barn boards for a floor. This leaden thing we dragged down to the beach and shoved into the water. It did not float high but it bore our combined weight and was not dangerously tippy. We paddled it around the lake with great effort, drifted into banks overhung with huge hemlock trees where beaver trails began and where we could reach out and pick huckleberries. We were so satisfied with ourselves and bragged to such excess that the next thing we knew Stephen and Peter had shamelessly begun their own raft. It was a hurriedly constructed affair, not nearly as seaworthy as ours, and made of very heavy green logs. When they launched it they barely floated at water level and appeared unstable.

"Hey Les, wanna have a war on the rafts?" queried Stephen hopefully after he and Peter dragged their raft to the water's edge.

"No, we don't want to have a war...dumb boys!" I muttered under my breath to Cynthia.

"Come on, Les. PLEASE !" Stephen insisted. "It's the thing to do. Really! You know what - we'll get buckets of mud and see who stays on their raft the longest...PLEASE! It'll be so much fun! A real Mud fight! Come on, Les!"

Since we noticed with satisfaction that the boy's raft was extremely tippy, it looked like a deal too good to pass up.

"What do you think, Cynth? I suppose we could wallop them."

"Gosh Les, I dunno..." Cynthia sounded tentative, but not totally resistant to the idea..

"This is going to be a piece of cake, Cynth!" I said smugly, my courage and vengeful spirit mounting.

"Yeah, let's get those creeps!" shouted Cynthia, suddenly enthusiastic for yet another collision with the boys. At least this time we would not be taken by surprise and everything looked on the up and up.

We gathered slimy creek mud in buckets, got mother and father to watch from the shore as referees, and paddled out to the middle of the lake. When we were within two yards of one another's raft we began to lob blobs of mud at each other. It was not easy to aim carefully or to stay afloat. If we both got on one side of the raft that side began to sink while the other side rose out of the water. The tendency was to over-compensate by running to the other side. This got the raft into a wildly rocking motion. All the while we were trying to duck and throw mud blobs. The boys and their raft began to sink as they tipped crazily from one side to the other. Finally they tipped so high the raft flipped upside down and they went overboard. Cynthia and I, balancing precariously on our raft became the winners, to our mud splattered delight. But the boys had looked awfully funny in their defeat and that counted for a lot with us. We could not help but feel a certain fondness for Stephen and Peter even though it was often with difficulty and necessitated a large measure of compassion and forgiveness. They each had a great sense of humor and their laughter was often directed at themselves.

Dry Sugar Falls

Dry Sugar Falls was a heavenly swimming hole. To get to it we had to park the car at the edge of a pasture and climb over a fence onto an old railroad trestle that spanned a deep ravine. This was scary because you could see between the railroad ties and straight down to the flat shale river bed. You had to always wonder if a train might come just as you got to the middle. Once on the other side we followed the river around a bend and deep into a canyon, at the end of which was a waterfall and a large deep pool of foaming warm water. It was like an exquisite natural bubble bath. The lower part of the falls was slippery and we would lie down in the cascading water and slide into the pool below. The water below was so soft we had the sensation of melting as we floated in it.

One fine day Mother, Cynthia and I went for a picnic to Dry Sugar Falls with Mr. Wilson, a well known writer friend of whom we were very fond, who spent his summers near Boonville. He did not drive, so when we arrived at his great stone house to pick him up, Mother had us jump out and go knock on the door. He rummaged behind the screen for his walking stick, and came out onto the front porch dressed in a battered hat, an old tweed jacket, short brown swim trunks and leather walking shoes. Now this was typical Upstate gear for a picnic and nothing to remark on. What caused Cynthia and me to gasp and our thirteen year old eyes to bulge nearly out of their sockets was his pink *whangdoodle** hanging down beside one leg. The swim trunks had no liner and he was stout enough not to be able to see below his stomach. He had no idea that he was indiscreetly exposed.

When he got into the car there it was again snuggled on his leg, and now two little *balls* were accompanying it. We were aghast. Mother chatted with him pleasantly, got the car started and turned around to us. She leaned over and quickly whispered, "Now girls, just don't pay any attention. Pretend it's not there. Just don't *look!*" So that is what we tried to do the best we could. We breathed deeply, tripped over rocks and tried to be interested in the natural beauty above and to either side but not below or near Mr. Wilson's legs. We tried hard to think about literary topics during the course of that peculiar picnic. But every now and then we found ourselves unintentionally looking to see if his *whangdoodle* was still hanging there. We didn't mean to look but we couldn't help ourselves. Sure enough, there it was. When we took him home late that afternoon, we remained silent and stunned in the car until we got home. Then as Mother recounted the tale to Father we exploded crazily, danced wildly, and wept with relief.

**whangdoodle* - n., a mythological creature with undefined characteristics; from Webster's New World Dictionary

Oh, To Be Naked!

Now more than ever before, Cynthia and I sought a delicious privacy. Our bodies were supple, sunny and bursting with health. We felt best in the barest amount of clothing, but it had to be completely comfortable and we did not wish to be observed. We loved to be naked. To be safely naked we had to wait until both the boys and mother and father went off to town. Then we could strip off our clothes, throw them with abandon over our shoulders and plunge into the lake to feel the icy water without clinging suits, to feel it luxuriously everywhere, in every nook and cranny, and then emerge to drip dry in the sun. We grabbed rackets and played badminton on the lawn, yelling as the spirit moved, or we walked naked in the woods. There was a titillating sensation about nakedness that was like quenching a long thirst. We felt at these times so beautiful and easy. The days were perfect as long as no one interfered. Without clothing we stretched and expanded in the sun. On long days when no one else was at home we made elaborate lunches with coleslaw and ate nakedly and ravenously, dipping into the center bowl with our fingers, dribbling cabbage onto our small breasts and giggling across from one another. At night we conspired to sleep naked in our small twin beds, and often late at night or before dawn we stole down to the pond to slip into the dark and cold water. These swims were eerie because the water was so black, but they tingled the skin, as well as the heart. We felt renewed. Emerging from the chilly waters was a supremely freshening experience.

Because we had resident beaver it was not unusual to see them in these nocturnal hours. They were on serious errands of their own, carrying twigs and alder branches back to their house. Beyond slapping their tails once or twice in warning, they usually continued about their food gathering chores sternly disregarding us. We, in contrast, looked on them with a near holy reverence and gratitude. Their existence on our pond was endlessly intriguing. They constantly made new canals by damming up the creek and diverting water to flood dry flat terrain. We loved to explore the newly made canals, and even dove down to their house entrance under the water when they were out. It was splendid to think that they lived in an actual house and maintained an entire world alongside ours as complicated and social as our own, but under the water.

Afternoons, Cynthia and I often canoed up the lake past a cattail swamp where there sunbathed a big box turtle, where we found duck eggs hidden in the grass and heard bullfrogs "gunking." We were at these times in an enchanted state. Wild fragrances wafted to us irresistibly and absorbed us in day dreams. We would paddle up the stream poling around new dams, hunching over as we slid past overhanging alder and azalea bushes. Trout hung nearly motionless in the deeper eddies behind the beaver dams and under sunken logs. At some point we would feel the pull to become one with the stream, and tie the canoe to a branch. The water was colder upstream but the desire to be submerged like the trout and the beaver, to be inside the dream, drifting along with our bodies in the stream was overwhelming. We would leave our clothes in the canoe and just float along with the current. The bottom was sandy and sparkled goldenly in the sunlight. Now and then we would float over an icy spot, an indication of a natural spring seeping up beneath the water.

One serene afternoon as we were drifting nakedly along we heard a snuffling in the bushes. Cynthia murmured, "Some animal is nearby, Les."

We each came slowly out of our reverie, thinking of the possibilities. It might be a deer with fawn. Or an industrious beaver, or even an otter, or perhaps a muskrat. Or a porcupine. Less likely, it might be a red fox, or just maybe the black bear that hibernated under a boulder in the woods behind the swamp. Cynthia mused out loud, "Les, what if it's the bear?"

I assured her nervously that it was not, and that even if it was, we would be O.K. But as the snuffling and crunching of twigs became louder and nearer I changed my mind. The thing was moving about very close to us now and we became alarmed. We had drifted around the bend, quite a ways from the canoe and our clothes.

Suddenly there was a great roar and two black lumps crashed out from the bushes, splashing into the water towards us. Our hearts fairly stopped for a second, before we realized that this racket was all just Stephen and Peter covered in mud. They had bushwhacked up the swamp, smeared themselves with mud, then stalked us up the creek. They had wanted us to think they were bears and give us a good fright - which they had - but of course they also couldn't resist the idea of spying on us. They were quite scratched from creeping and crawling stealthfully through all those bushes and they were very uncomfortable as the mud was beginning to dry over their faces, hair and clothing. Due to their own discomfort our nakedness was somewhat overlooked. They bathed themselves as we retrieved our clothing and the canoe, and then we gave them a lift back to camp. They had gone to so much trouble that we naturally if a trifle grudgingly forgave them for spoiling our privacy.

Stephen and Peter were imaginative and relentless in their preoccupation with us because we were girls, and this preoccupation manifested in strange and humorous bumblings. We were not boyfriends and girlfriends in any sense, nor were we really sibling rivals any longer. We were someplace in between, which enabled us to have adjoining bedrooms and swim together sometimes in our underwear when we had forgotten our swimsuits, and to play boisterous card games and croquet with childish enjoyment. Cynthia and I were two years younger and our pubescence was markedly less obtrusive than Stephen and Peter's. While we enjoyed eating, we did not need a half gallon of milk with four hamburgers at a sitting and three slices of apple pie for dessert. Both boys, in spite of becoming more fun to be with, had insatiable appetites coupled with a provoking flatulence which they plainly enjoyed.

Rites of Passage

At midsummer, the boys were dropped off with a canoe and backpacks to travel through the chain lakes by themselves as a rite of passage. Cynthia and I were naturally jealous but overjoyed to see them paddling into the sunset. We could scarcely believe the peace and quiet back at camp. The first few days we spent just breathing deeply, swimming naked, and stretching to fill all the spaces their absence had created. By the end of the week it was almost too quiet.

Unobserved, Cynthia and I meandered down the road towards town. It was a hot, still afternoon and there was the sweet fragrance of pine needles as we sauntered along. We came to an overgrown driveway and turned into it, searching for wild blackberries. At the end of the driveway, partially covered with honeysuckle vines was a small two-story house. It was obvious that no one was home or had lived there for some time. It had that certain look of having been abandoned and forgotten.

We climbed the leaning front stairs onto a small porch and peered through the kitchen window. There was a tattered lace curtain but we could see a wooden kitchen table with place settings for two, silverware, glass mugs, a half smoked cigar and a jar of pickles. Alongside the table against the far wall was a cabinet with crockery and glasses stored inside. We peered through the living room window and saw a small couch, a braided rug and a few small chairs and an end table. It was a modest house with neither running water nor electricity.

Shyly we pushed open the door and then, as in a dream, we were both standing inside with the door shut and our heartbeat in our throats. We were in a stranger's house, and nobody else in the entire world knew this. We each took a place at the table and sat down, examined the pickles, and noted that there was also a pack of cards resting on the table.

"They must have been playing cards, and then they just got up and left in the middle of dinner and they never came back." I said. Cynthia agreed, tasting a pickle.

"I'm going to deal you a hand now," I said, picking up the pack of cards. "It's going to be winner takes all."

There was a slight drawl creeping into my voice. Cynthia immediately looked my way, and her eyes got squinty.

"Wall, that suits me fine, but this time keep your hands above the table where I can see them, or there'll be trouble!"

"That's just fine by me," I answered, "and the exact same goes for you, Hombre."

I dealt her five cards, and myself five and put the rest in the center and turned one face up. She fanned her cards and yawned. Then she selected three from her hand and put them face down. "I'll take three," she said, and helped herself.

"I'll take one," I muttered, "and I'll...hmmm...I'll raise you my horse."

"Wall, you cain't scare me!" she drawled. "I'll see you

my painted stallion and half the gold in my saddlebags from that last job we did down in Dallas."

I looked at her with steely eyes, dead sober, and drew on the half smoked cigar butt that I'd found lying on the edge of my plate. "I'll see you all that gold in MY bags and raise you my pearl handled pistol"!

She fell silent at this, for she knew that particular pistol to be a priceless family heirloom, very likely stolen from under the pillow of a famous outlaw by my great grand-mother as he lay dying of gunshot wounds in the heart.

"Now I'm gonna see you with my double barreled shotgun, the one that I personally use to kill anyone that gits in my way, and that's the last word I'm goin' ter say ter youse, Sidewinder!" Cynthia drawled menacingly.

We lay down our hands. Cynthia had clearly won.

"Why you double crossing Hyena!" I exclaimed. "I would have won, but I saw you snatch a card from under the table and you know just how I feel about that!"

"I most certainly did not!" Cynthia retorted.

"You calling me a liar?" I countered dangerously.

"I ain't callin' you nothin' but a yellow bellied wart hog!" she sneered. "And I didn't cheat!"

"You better say that with a smile 'cus I'm beginning to git ornery now," I hissed, "and I don't aim to let no low life skum sucking salamander cheat on me an git away with it!"

Cynthia remarked, "Oh yeah?" and tipped the jar of pickles over towards me. The juice ran under my plate and dripped onto my lap. As I jumped to my feet the whole table upended with everything clattering to the floor - pickles, plates, mugs, cards, soggy cigar. Cynthia screamed and grabbed her chair and I grabbed mine and we tussled, viciously whacking the chairs together. They were old and frail and they splintered easily. She screamed again, pleased with the sound.

"Now I'm gonna have to kill you right here on the spot 'cus I cain't take no more sass you understand," I panted and then I chased her up the stairs to the bedroom. We discovered bedding and pillows which we threw at each other until the room was snowing in feathers. We chased around shrieking with delight and jumping on beds covered in feathers until we were nearly sick with exhaustion and laughter. Then we crept down the stairs and left the house like thieves, closing the door carefully behind us. We felt guilty for being so destructive, but at the same time we were curiously elated to hold such a terrible secret. We were bound together now in wickedness and we compensated at home by being especially cheerful and helpful with the dishes and little chores we had heretofore put off. It was both awful and wonderful to have mother treat us the same as yesterday, completely ignorant of our combined depravity.

On the following afternoon we sauntered once again down the road, and once more furtively went up the little overgrown driveway to the abandoned house. It was just as we had left it. The table was tipped over and there was smashed crockery on the floor among fat old pickles and broken chair legs. Feathers had drifted down the stairs and lay fluffily at the bottom.

Cynthia whispered, "Gosh, Les, look what we've done!"

"It's pretty bad, all right!" I agreed.

"Shouldn't we fix it up?" she wondered aloud, as she bent over and picked up a splintered chair. We looked around and were still astonished by the discovery of this house of treasure.

"Look at all the stuff just left here! Glasses and furniture and everything!" She went over and balanced a tureen in her hands.

"Oops!" It suddenly dropped from her hands and

smashed on the floor. "Oh no! Oh my gosh, Les!" she exclaimed with genuine alarm, and then a rapturous look came over her face.

We helped ourselves to the remaining dishes, bowls and glassware in the cabinet and dropped them piece by piece onto the floor where they smashed as they hit other pieces.

"Ouch!" a small bowl landed on my foot. "Hey, you did that on purpose, Cynthia!"

"No I did not!" she cried honestly.

"Well, I'm going to have to get you back anyway!"

Cynthia screamed and ran for the stairs and I chased after her. At the top she grabbed and threw a small chair down the stairs. I ducked and it hit the wall behind me. One leg tip stuck in the wall. This was amazing. The chair just hung there stuck in the wall.

"Wowie, Les! How bout this?" she shrieked and then sent another chair right through the upstairs window.

"Yippie!" I yelled heaving out a small end table. We shredded sheets, overjoyed at the dreadful tearing sound, then raced downstairs and tossed all the furniture we could lift out the windows, shattering all the glass panes downstairs.

Finally we were spent, so we again closed the door with great care and crept down the driveway, turned onto the road and soberly walked home, glancing occasionally over our shoulders. We felt even more guilty and destructive than before. That evening as we sat stricken and silent in the living room, I said, "Mom, what happens when kids get caught wrecking other people's property?" She answered pleasantly, without even pausing to consider, "Oh, I imagine the police come and take them away to jail."

That did it. I was positive that the police were going to come at any moment and take us away, mortified, guilty beyond forgiveness, our futures ruined, taken off to be publicly displayed in jail. This dreadful fear of being

100

caught, coupled with the agonizing wish that we had never discovered that house took the sunshine out of two days of our lives. Both of us just sat, or dragged ourselves around listlessly. Waiting... On the third day however, when the police still had not come for us, the need to just see the house again became ever stronger, and we once more found ourselves meandering back down the road to turn into the little driveway, and once again we climbed up the leaning stairs past the debris of broken crockery and furniture and entered the kitchen door.

The whole interior was a shambles. It belonged only to us. We began where we had left off, screaming and tearing at curtains and kicking holes in the walls as though we were having fits. The innocence of the first day was gone, that first day of discovery with its intensity of pleasure and imagination. We now mostly just felt wicked. Ghoulishly we completed what we had begun, sickened but unable to stop.

When the boys returned from their fabulous canoe trip the following day, we were glad and relieved to show them all that we had accomplished in their absence. Our private experience had been heady, even erotic. Stephen and Peter were genuinely impressed. They played at the ruined house themselves for a few days, but we did not join them. We were satiated at last with the whole rotten business. They diffused our guilt somewhat by breaking a few things that we had overlooked. No one came back to that house before it caved in. A few years later it was bull-dozed.

We girls had no sanctioned ritual or signposts from our elders, no rites of passage. We were not allowed to go off to prove ourselves, presumably for safety reasons. It was assumed we did not need any special pubescent rite of passage because we were girls and would just naturally grow up lovely. Ho Ho. Double Ha.

Saturdays in Town

Late Saturday afternoons we all piled into the Buick, fondly called the "Green Gopher," and drove in to have supper at Jess and John's house. Their neighbor Charlie was likely to be sitting on an apple crate behind the barn drinking himself into a stupor. From the time I was little I was horribly fascinated by the dreadful sight of this bloodshot-eyed woeful man. He was perhaps handsome in his youth and he tried to be a good neighbor, but he was a ruined soul. He began his career as a policeman; however, his drunkenness had caused his demotion to local dog catcher. We once watched him sitting with a pretty stray collie, one that he was ordered to destroy. He drank himself into a near coma, then shoved the dog into the trunk of his car, slammed the lid down, loaded his rifle and drove to the dump where he planned to shoot it. After this incident in which I never forgot the pleading look on the dog's face as the trunk lid came down, I was unable to look at Charlie without a shudder of revulsion. He was a pathetic monster, yet Jessie had a peaceful way with him and said he was a good neighbor.

After dinner on Saturday night we all strolled to the

village square where the local "Old Timer's Band" was setting up in the ornate bandstand and where families sat about on the park benches or in folding chairs on the grass. There were always some who stayed in their pickups parked along the curb with the windows rolled down. Women often had their hair in curlers, even though this was their Saturday night outing. I supposed they did this in order to look their best at Sunday church, but it struck me as peculiar since it was, after all, Saturday night. Since many women did watch the band concert in curlers it was apparently an acceptable custom - perhaps even a style.

At the park we were likely to see Luther Fox, an enormously fat and simple minded man who lived over the hat shop. He would lean on a parking meter and say friendly things to people passing by, things you couldn't help but agree with. "Nice evening, eh?" he might say, to which you would reply, "Ehyah, surely is." Local folks were pleasant to him as well as to Paul Kirk, the other simple soul who was as thin as Luther was fat. While Luther delivered a limited number of newspapers about town for his daily work, Paul never went anywhere without his push mower. Often he appeared to be mowing the sidewalk in front of the village post office. As he came alongside a parked car, if the window was rolled down, he would stick his head deep inside, nearly nose to nose, and carefully scrutinize the occupants. "Think it's gonna rain?" he generally asked no matter what the weather suggested. It was his number one topic of conversation. He would scratch his head quizzically before frowning, shaking his head and muttering that it was definitely "gonna rain." Then he would pull his head back out of the window and with one hand twisting his shirt button the other would push the lawn mower on down the sidewalk.

One winter, enormous Luther developed pneumonia. He slowly squeezed up the back stairs to his tiny room over the hat shop and went to bed. People became concerned

103

and a doctor was fetched. It was decided that he needed to be taken to the hospital. Since it was impossible to carry him back down the narrow stairs, men brought a crane and then dismantled the front windows and removed the window casings. They tried to squeeze him through the opening. They meant to lift him down with the crane. He died stuck there, half in and half out of the window.

Another remarkably fat, enterprising man you were bound to see on Saturday night was Mr. Fitz, the undertaker. He had a popcorn machine which he wrestled out to the curb. Wearing his stained white teeshirt that did not quite cover his stomach, he filled and sold red and white bags of popcorn for ten cents. Kids climbed on the World War I cannon while everyone chatted and felt the slow, golden pleasure of a secure summer evening. Eventually the band struck up a Sousa march and played other popular marches for about an hour. At the end of each piece everyone clapped, whistled shrilly or honked their horns in appreciation. Kids marched around as if they were going to war and chased each other. We were very proud that Jessie's father Clark played his tuba with the band. His was the "umpa pa" part and you could easily hear it at the bottom of everything. These evenings were perfect because we went as a family and mingled with the whole community in this informal celebration. I recall Saturday nights as among the few times I felt that I was truly an American and that this is what that word described.

Other nights we occasionally went to town to see a movie at the Franjo Theater, a typical American small town movie house with the neon billboard out front, and stiff burgundy horsehair chairs inside. The movies were invariably either westerns or monster movies. We could resist the monsters but not the westerns due to my father's romantic nature and his reverence for the Old West. But most nights we stayed home and played cards or read long, complicated novels of romance and adventure which we gathered from the village library shelves in tall piles and carted home. Our house had many comfortable reading chairs and we were all strong readers. We often sat late into the night bowed over our private books, coming up for air only when someone broke the spell by popping a bowl of corn.

When we retired, it was to the strains of the whippoorwill calling its lonesome tune from the roof top, and the endless rolling song of Mile creek as it cascaded over the dam. These sounds came to me as the strains of deeply serene isolation. We were a summer family enfolded safely in our well worn cozy farmhouse, encircled by the dark, vibrant forest, nourished by our lake's eternal waters.

Differences

Inevitably there came a season when Cynthia and I were not enough for each other. We did not know this matter of factly. We sensed it by a degree of frustration between ourselves and an availability to other friends that had not been there before. We each always had other friendships and enjoyed them in the ongoing way of having someone over for Friday or Saturday night. Sleep-overs were very natural and important. Around ninth grade we passed into a new phase of friendship in which we sometimes hurt one another's feelings. We were each becoming more distinctly separate people, with differences of opinion regarding how best to grow up.

Cynthia was intrigued and glad to be turning into a woman. She looked forward to wearing lipstick and painting her nails bright red or subtle shades of pink. She genuinely enjoyed preening and dress styles and make-up. And she already had all this paraphernalia at home belonging to her older sisters. She cajoled me into shaving my legs by purchasing me a feminine razor for Christmas, and along with her I began to worry about obtaining glossy hair by using creme rinses. I did want to be attractive and acceptable. On the other hand there was a part of me that wanted an alternative to all thís, that observed it all as a horrid trap and an ending to the perfect understanding of life that I perceived we had. Really, what was happening was that Cynthia wanted to go ahead and enjoy growing up in our culture. She did not especially have a bone to pick with it; she was not a rebel or dissenter by nature. And she was basically a happy person. She was tired of being opposed to progress, tired of my politics of separatism. Had there been a choice in women's "schools of becoming," we would have chosen differently. She was really not confused, and I was. I cannot say that there was anyone that I wished to emulate, unless it was Auntie Mame, and admittedly she was a fictional character. Nor did I have a mentor. All of my developed senses of strength appeared to be undermined by the feminization of girls occurring at school. I began to shut down, to speak out less and to be attracted to the more radically introverted girls - the ones so out of it through ugliness or intellect that they made no effort to integrate. Cynthia, on the other hand, was attracted to the outgoing, socially more well adjusted and defined girls.

One day Cynthia asked me if I minded if she became another girl's best friend. This came out of the blue and I was crushed, but behaved with what I meant to be nonchalance. "Of course not, Cynthia", I answered. "I'm really more interested in Sarah these days anyway. We have so much more in common."

Cynthia pushed harder. "You know Les, you will always be my Snookum X, but Ginny really wants me to be her best friend because she really needs someone to talk to. But I wanted to ask you before I made my decision."

I was wounded, and said bitterly, "That's fine with me, if it's what you want. I don't really care!" and hung up.

I could not look squarely at just how wounded I felt

over Cynthia's choosing another friend over me. The issue appeared to be whether or not I was still lovable. If Cynthia didn't love me anymore, then probably nobody loved me. At the same time I was not altogether focused on my friendship with Cynthia. I was fascinated and drawn towards the older radical beatniks and the pacifists that I saw at the coffee houses and was branching out in my own fashion.

That, however, didn't count. What counted was her changing her feelings about me. I did not analyze what she said or try to understand her point of view. It was too mortifying to look at clearly, or to discuss with her, and my foremost reaction was to cover my feelings and to appear nonchalant - hopefully even to pull away first so that I wasn't nakedly left behind to drop into a black and sightless pit where I might cease to exist. If Cynthia did not value me, then I might actually be of no value. My protection was now gone and I was out there in the world - on the front lines of chaos without a buddy.

Jean-Paul Sartre's books "Existentialism" and "La Nausea" sat on my desk. As I read them I became despairing and slightly nauseated. I sank into the dark pointlessness of my existence. This was not altogether unpleasant. It made me kin to great philosophers, poets, and writers. My depression gave way to creative urgency. I became glumly excited. I went on a reading and writing binge and felt solitary, yes, but now I was fomenting with unrealized potential. I was going to *create* a meaningful existence.

A week later there was a surprise birthday party for me, of all people, and Cynthia contrived to get me to it. I was mortified because I was not feeling very loving or generous towards any of my old friends. I assumed nobody much liked me either; furthermore, Greg was there with his new pretty girl friend, which made me grumpy, and the whole party seemed ridiculous. While it was undoubtedly conceived out of the desire for friendship, it appeared to me, under the circumstances, artificial, collusive, and cruel. I was given a huge stuffed Snoopy dog, which had everybody's signature on it. This was about like being given a plaster leg cast in my broody opinion. I had to wrestle with myself not to throw the dumb thing on the floor and burst into tears. I assumed that Cynthia and I would at least go home together since we had arrived together. But she had already made plans to spend the night with Ginny, her new best friend. My heart sank to an all-time low. I felt betrayed, warty and ugly. I could not think of anybody I liked, least of all myself.

Thereafter I did become good friends with Sarah, a deeply introverted Catholic girl who taught me to say "Hail Mary" and intrigued me with her religious intensity. She was going to become a nun, and that seemed very desirable to both of us, although I, being faithless, had a longer, perhaps endless row to hoe. Sarah was kind, but to some extent distant and preoccupied. At least she was not boy crazy or treacherous. She wore strange, brown monklike clothing that I wished I owned and could also wear.

Cynthia's older sister Polly was also a deeply introverted girl who loved flowers and kept mostly to herself. Her father in his concern for her built her a small glass greenhouse where she potted flowers and spent much of her time. She and I began to be friends, to Cynthia's bewilderment. Because she was completely out of the mainstream social life at school and seemed to think for herself, and because she was actually wonderful in her humor and her eccentricity, as well as generous hearted, and BEST of all, because she seemed to be fond of me, we became good friends over time. One day I thoughtlessly suggested that we meet at the white picket fence to begin a long afternoon walk.

Unbeknownst to either of us Cynthia eavesdropped on

the conversation. Wrapping herself in her father's over-coat she trailed behind Polly to find out where she was going. As Polly and I hailed one another at the fence, Cynthia suddenly emerged from the bushes, furious and outraged.

"You horrible Snookum!" she yelled. "Traitor! I hate you, you TRAITOR!" Then she shrieked, "How could you be so mean! I HATE YOU, DO YOU HEAR?"

Stricken and sobbing, she turned and fled home. I ran after her, shocked and surprised at what I had done, and touched by her reaction. I found her sobbing behind her parent's locked bedroom door. I pleaded with her but she would not come out.

"I hate you! Go home you traitor! You're not my *friend* anymore." Then brokenly, she sobbed, "Les, how could you!"

Wonderingly, with a small shaft of sunlight filtering into my hardened brain, I said, "But I thought Ginny was your best friend - that it didn't matter anymore." But I understood that indeed it did matter and that I had betrayed our secret world that had never been opened to anyone else. The fabric of that world still gave us strength and integrity.

Although we did make up, and went out and had many other friends, some very close, all very important, we never again confused what was sacred between us, in our lives as children.

High School

Through high school Cynthia and I continued to be connected in spite of our growing differences. In tenth grade my family went back to Europe for another year. Mother and father lived in Italy and Stephen and I were placed in an expensive boarding school in Switzerland - one which we were excited about. However, the moment the train pulled away, carrying Mother and Father to Italy, I sank into the desolate feelings of being eight years old again. I plunged into the familiar old helpless emotions of despair and grief. How confusing, because Stephen and I had spent months anticipating this new experience! Yet there I was again, and I could do nothing about my homesickness except live with it and wait for the aching in my throat to leave.

After some weeks the grief subsided and I was able to look around. Stephen and I were housed in separate buildings but we shared classes and meals in a converted chateau. We made an effort to eat together and were allies once more. Unfortunately it was only a short time before it became obvious that the school was not academically challenging but rather a place for very rich Americans to deposit unwanted children. As soon as I realized this I determined that the two of us were not going to stay there.

We did not belong. This time I was older and eloquent enough to sound convincing. Nevertheless it took five months of letters and determination before Mother and Father agreed to let us come and live with them. And so we happily gathered our belongings and caught a train to join them in Italy. Once there we enjoyed ourselves immensely for a month before packing up and moving with them to France. There Mother and Father did not have room for us in their prearranged flat. Undaunted, Stephen and I found our own lodging on the top floor of a modest hotel located on a narrow market street a few blocks away. We break-fasted together in the lobby, chatting over bowls of hot cocoa and croissants, then bicycled off to our separate schools. In France boys and girls our age were kept well apart during adolescence. We saw our parents for dinner each night. This was a satisfying arrangement and I was content. We were experiencing an unusual measure of independence, facing strange schools, people and situa-tions entirely on our own in a foreign country, but we did speak the language and we had each other. Best of all Mother and Father were not far away. Of course I did feel alone and different from my new French friends, but that was acceptable, and even a little romantic. Life on my own was far better than being in a boarding school. I now had a measure of self determination, and a bicycle, and every day was interesting. When I was not doing school work I explored the fascinating side streets of the town, read Andre Maurois and Colette, and on pretty days bicycled with a picnic to the surrounding countryside, which was the beautiful Loire valley.

One afternoon I came early to my parents flat and saw a letter addressed to them from our next door neighbors at home. They had agreed to keep Bootsie during our ab-sence. I quickly scanned the letter searching for news of her. There was the usual information about the weather and about home canning, and some neighborly gossip and then the following sentence:

"As we agreed earlier, I had the Vet put Bootsie to sleep. She was not especially happy and was proving to be a nuisance."

I reread the sentence. Then I read it again. I could not make any sense out of it. In the silence of the room the words ricocheted across my brain. Reality exploded. The fact of Bootsie's murder was not possible - adults could not behave this way! I wanted to strike them. I wanted to bludgeon down the walls with my outraged pain! Who in the world were my mother and father anyway? What kind of people would sanction such a thing? In that moment, at the deepest level, I lost my ability to trust.

My white, hot useless anger I vented on Mother as soon as she walked in the door. As often happened when Mother found herself suddenly in a corner, she got mad at me for being stubborn and willful. The ugly fact of Bootsie's death just sat there with no place to go. The best I could do was vow wrathfully that I would never, ever abandon a pet of mine once I was on my own.

In June we returned to Boonville for the summer. Cynthia flew there to spend a few weeks before meeting up with her family on their way to winter in Scotland. She was by now beginning to lengthen out and she had passed me in height. She was becoming noticeably gorgeous, with raven black hair. We had a splendid time together, swimming, playing tennis, mixing in with a group of Boonville kids our age for many picnics and outings. We double dated village boys and felt altogether desirable and full of ourselves. It was not a time of deep philosophical talks but rather a prolonged dance in the summer sunshine.

Before leaving she instructed me in the new friends she had made back at school in California and insisted on my being friendly to them. She had already left them instructions to take me in hand when I arrived in the fall. It turned out they were the popular pom-pom girls for the football team and they did welcome me into their circle, thus expanding my popularity considerably for as long as I could maintain an interest in football, boys on the football team, tight skirts, phone calls from boys I did not want to date, parties I was uncomfortable at - for the sake of appearing to be popular. One day I had enough of it all and descended the ugly old stairs to the seedy cafeteria where all the intellectual nerds hung out. There were my old friends from grade school, munching their sandwiches and laughing uproariously over something. It was the laughter that got to me. It was not meant to sound enticing - it just was. I sat down and had the best genuine fun I'd had in ages, and thereafter I began riding my bike to school and being my old strange self again.

Cynthia returned from Scotland having learned the Highland Fling. She brought me a beautiful hand made kilt. She renewed her friendship with the popular girls and managed in her uniquely generous spirited way to also keep all her old friends as well.

We studied for our driver's licences together. For this event we borrowed Uncle Bert's small car, figuring that we would have a better chance of parallel parking with it. Cynthia went first and passed the test without a hitch. I was very anxious and drove straight through a red light at a busy intersection of the highway, giving the examiner a nasty scare, and flunked. This was so mortifying that I was unable to remain at school that day. Mother thoughtfully came and picked me up. I was a sobbing wreck. The next morning, before school, Cynthia went with me back to the examiner and I passed. She never gloated one bit over getting her license first, but when her father heard about the event, he was tickled.

The week before Christmas I was driving us down the highway in rush hour traffic. Cynthia and I were shopping for a Christmas tree, and as we sped along I became aware that the only thing keeping the cars in the opposite lane was a *painted* line. The more I thought about this the more insane it seemed. We were all barely missing total chaos, collision and certain death because of a *painted* line. I just had to pull over, close my eyes and let Cynthia drive.

Cynthia never faltered from her original intention to become a nurse. In college she was a serious nursing student. She went steady with a fraternity boy who was to become a lawyer and her future husband. I became intimate with an old school friend named Ralph. We were both theater students and conscientious objectors of the Vietnam War. Feelings from my childhood were burbling up leaving me confused and wounded. Stephen's and my abandonment in Europe and Bootsie's murder remained unresolved. I turned toward Ralph for safety and understanding. Mother and father fiercely disapproved of Ralph. Upon graduation, Cynthia had an enormous wedding. I eloped. At Cynthia's wedding shower all the girls giggled and were happy. I felt uncomfortably out of place. I hardly knew Cynthia anymore. We had gone so far apart I could not identify with her friends or her pleasure at all. I saw any part of the establishment as hypocritical and self serving, and I wanted to get far away from it all: university, parents, the pentagon, cities, roads, most people. When Ralph and I left for Alaska in an old jeep truck, I really did not plan on ever looking back.

Wisdom of The Aged Ones

Ten years went by. Cynthia practiced her nursing, had three children, and settled with her family in Washington D.C.. Ralph and I completed two years of service work with retarded children and went on to become Alaskan film makers. Seven years and many remarkable adventures down the road I abandoned the marriage. The reasons were murky and it was without a sense of fairness. Although I deeply cared about Ralph I felt trapped and out of my own skin. Marriage triggered behavior patterns in me that did not even marginally represent who I was. The day after our marriage I purchased an iron and got us both new underwear. Ralph was as shocked as I was. Later when I threw off all the imprinted duties and vows I felt guilty and shameful and selfish. I had to believe that it was better for me to let go and brave the tumultuous waters of life on my own terms, reflecting my own ideas of reality. It was past time for me to shake out and live my own life.

It took years of sometimes messy experience, loneliness, reflection, and the shock of Cynthia's cancer to reckon with myself and look homeward. I had become devastatingly self critical. Furthermore, I was in the negative process of perceiving myself as a victim. Although now a successful artist, I saw myself as mostly a failure. I felt like I was amounting to nothing, that everyone was disappointed in me, and that I was even visibly shrinking. Springtime which had always before been joyous and full of promise, now merely emphasized my loneliness and my despair. I began to experience an overwhelming disappointment in the life I had created. The problem was that I refused to play the culturally sanctioned role, yet I had not really *endorsed* any alternative choice. Where were all the promises, the laughter, and the joy? What did I have to look forward to, having squandered my opportunities for family, children, and even a normal career? As I started slipping down into self criticism and despair, I could not stop. When I struggled back to the surface, I felt a fatigue such as I had never known.

Loving friends were there for me. And so were mother and father. One winter when I was struggling alone mother sent me a pair of hand knit slippers she had made, and inside the toe of one was tucked a hundred dollar bill. It was just there nestled in the warmth of cozy slippers. Mother made sure I had enough money to live that winter, and she never suggested how to spend the money or talked about it at all. Another time while visiting them in Boonville I suddenly began to weep at the breakfast table. My father rose from his chair and came behind me, placed his hands on my shoulders, then stooped and kissed the top of my head. Slow as a turtle I began to undergo an attitude shift and gave myself permission to be myself. And I went looking for good experiences.

Eventually I began to feel right. I had learned to care for myself, and I now understood that Mother and father had always loved me and done their best *at the time*. I stopped picking over old bones. The more I thought about them, the more I was glad they were my parents. I even became positively grateful. If it hadn't been for their on-going devoted friendship with Cynthia's parents, Cynthia and I might have lost one another. Because our parents continued to walk together and visit, Cynthia and I always knew vicariously what was going on with each other. Our parents kept the circle for us.

We have often talked of our parents, of the elegance and grace with which they have lived and prospered in marriages that both have lasted over half a century. Certainly we each have our favorite stories of our parent's eccentricities. One of Cynthia's is of her mother standing on the small balcony over the kitchen holding a new Corning ware casserole dish, when Cynthia brought her college roommate home for the first time. Yvonne gaily greeted Cynthia, shouting down "Hello dear!" Cynthia, taking the situation in, rather nervously asked, "What are you doing, Mommy?" To which Yvonne joyfully replied, "I'm just testing this new Corning ware dish that I bought. It says on the box that it's absolutely unbreakable! Isn't that wonderful?" With that she dropped it over the railing and down onto the brick patio below, where it smashed into many fragments. Yvonne has always been a surprise to her family: colorful, brilliantly absentminded, temperamental and generous hearted, lovingly surrounded by devoted daughters and an ever-expanding family of relatives and friends.

Cynthia's father Sidney was dedicated to his medical research, but nevertheless devoted absolutely to his wife and five daughters. They in turn doted on him, and Cynthia lavished him with outright adoration when we were children. As he reached retirement age, he became an avid oil painter in the manner of Georges Seurat, and every now and then an enormous oil painting would appear in the house depicting sumptuous gatherings of French people who looked curiously like his own daughters on holiday picnics circa 1880.

My mother Mary carried a complex assortment of

traits: she had conservative midwestern views on ethics, money and morality, a tireless curiosity about all living creatures, an avid interest in botany, an ability to laugh until she both cried and wet her pants over strange behaviors and ridiculous events. She was sometimes excessively concerned with outward appearances to the neglect of deeper understandings. Although she always had trouble carrying a tune, she was a terrific dancer. She would occasionally break into the Charleston when the mood struck her.

One summer in Boonville, we drained our lake in order to have the cement dam resurfaced. My mother and I hiked halfway around it to explore the edges. We then decided to take the shortest way home which was through the middle. Since the bottom appeared very muddy we shed our clothes and started across in our underwear. The mud got deeper and thicker until we were up to our thighs and had to begin slithering along on our stomachs. We went the whole distance like two salamanders and as we puffed, wheezed and groaned with the effort, we also had fits of uproarious laughter. I was about fourteen at the time, and I remember saving that moment forever in my mind. It was of my mother and me laughing like two young girls, playing together and finding ourselves in an hilarious situation. I have since had many moments of silliness with her and each time is equally precious to my memory of her unbounded side, the side I most cherish, which is free of constraints and truly creative.

My father has always dressed for dinner and held doors for my mother. I have never heard him burp, much less say anything stronger than "Damn!" when angry or frustrated, even though he is undoubtedly temperamental by nature. He, like mother, has a keen curiosity and a wonderful ability to be silly. His self-centeredness, coupled with a brilliant analytical mind suggested a certain remoteness during my childhood, which my mother furthered and protected; however, his genuine innocence and outright honesty overshadowed this in later years, and his romantic nature and love of the out of doors made him affectionate to all creatures.

He was a fan of the Old West and bragged of having the flat belly of an Indian runner as well as of being the Fastest Gun in the West. In fact he was a sensitive pianist who in croquet games became fiercely competitive and was likely to tear his hair and fall to his knees moaning over defeat, or to leap into the air and prance, mallet waving proudly overhead in victory.

Cynthia came to Boonville many times after our first glorious summer together. We often sang over my father's shoulder while he played ragtime tunes and love songs on our old player piano in the living room - the same piano that we'd had at the Reverend's house, for he had given it to us as a house warming present. Our favorite summer song was *"Moonlight in Jungleland"*:

Moonlight in Jungleland
Moonlight and love
In the Jungle glade each monkey maid
Is somebody's turtle dove
Lovely Miss Kangaroo
Spoons on the sand
With a chimpanzee her affinity
When it's Moonlight In Jungleland!

Leaving Heaven

Mother and Father eventually retired from the university and moved permanently to Boonville where they productively enjoyed themselves for many years. Father became a photographer and mother continued with her painting - and together they began a recycling program for the community at the village landfill. As the seasons passed so did their oldest and dearest friends Clark and Hilda, Louie and Gracie and then lastly even Jess and John. Then one year the place seemed too much work for them. Stephen and I lived far away and neither of us were able to move or commute to Boonville. Mother and father decided it was time to say good-bye to the north country for good. Our camp was sold and they moved back to California to live within a short walk of Cynthia's parents.

This leave-taking of Boonville was very painful for all of us and signified in a sense, the end of the story that they had begun with their marriage. I cannot help but grieve that there are such endings, that all of life and wonderful stories are, after all, transitory. When I went for the last time to Boonville to say good-bye, I walked the woods, canoed on the lake, and daydreamed as before, only this time it was late fall and very quiet. I spent most of my time reminiscing.

How do I say good-bye to you motherland
everyone I ever loved reminds me of you
My father held me in
the deep Black River
my first frenzied dog paddle
Brother and I so small
we sat in the same slate pothole
catching crayfish, exploring
slippery trilobite patterns underfoot
while mother painted
our father fished

We were a summer family
crabbed in leaky innertubes
elbows skinned, bouncing, burbling
laughing, bobbing the rapids
calling out to each other
exuberant on our boisterous river

And Oh mighty Moose, your soft gold waters flow
sleekly, through rust streaked
granite canyons. I remember
leaping into your swirling depths
draping myself water-sated
over sunkissed, female smooth stone
eating watercress sandwiches and sinking
into dizzy long hot naps

Edges of tall blackskinned white pines
soft lashed needles shivering
pale chattering birch leaves
my barefoot dreamland here
a scented sandy carpet of moss
wintergreen, and huckleberry
a patch of secretive wild strawberries

How we loved Dry Sugar Falls
hidden in a cow pasture
lacy rivulets cascading downward
foamy petals of Baby's-breath strewn
on deep waters below
floating in your fragrance I muse
everyone I ever loved reminds me of you

In our own pond
spatterdock lilies and dragonflies
tickle the water surface
beavers swim nightly from their lodge
chew and irrigate the alder groves
design this land
fell logs, build dams
it is for all this
a moving landscape

My canoe drifts into the cattails
the bullfrogs Boom

Everyone I ever loved I dream of here
I have brought them with me and introduced you
and now they know you
just as mother and father brought one another home
every summer for fifty-two years
to remember how their love
their essential journey together
unfolded here
they never spoke this way
it was the way they lived

Every wild place I have known reminds me
you are my fertile, aqueous mother
my green, rainbow leaved, lightening mother
I can touch you and be home
wherever there is iridescent moss
and memory to stir.

EPILOGUE

After her last chemotherapy session Cynthia flew west to visit me. I was again living on my small green island in the Puget Sound. I was very pleased to see, upon her arrival, that in spite of her serious bout with cancer she was not too much the worse for wear. In fact her general enthusiasm and zest for life was an inspiration to me. I suggested (maniacally in retrospect) that we plan an adventurous outing to a neighboring island. Cynthia thought that an excellent idea. In fact she said I owed her an adventure.

So rather on the spur of the moment one afternoon we put a life jacket on Cynthia and I put on my garage sale shortie wet suit that was frog green and too small, and we headed over to an island state park in a pair of kayaks. The island was about three miles distant and when we arrived Cynthia was obviously tired and quite winded. Also it was late afternoon. We had an enjoyable stroll on shore and a bit of a rest. I needed to relieve myself so Cynthia got back into her kayak while I laboriously squeezed out of my wetsuit. There was probably only one other person on the entire island that day and he happened by at just that moment. Wetsuits are not easy to pull back on when they are wrapped around your ankles. It was so impossible to avoid being seen in this compromising position that Cynthia just burst out laughing. By the time I had climbed into my kayak I noticed that a wind had come up and the tide was running.

Almost immediately Cynthia confessed "Les, I'm too tired. I can't paddle any more."

Ever the optimist, I said stoutly, "No problem, Cynth," and grabbed a long piece of bull kelp, tied it to the bow of her kayak and the stern of mine, and said once again reassuringly, "No problem Cynthia, this is going to be a piece of cake!"

We got about halfway across with me towing her when I began to lose my stamina and the combination of the tidal current and the wind kept us from moving forward. It was all I could do to stay in the same spot and not drift backwards towards the mainland many miles away. Cynthia's head was drooping in serious fatigue. I was getting anxious, and wondered why I had blithely gotten us into this mess.

Then far across the sound, our neighbors started up their Boston whaler and headed towards us. They had sensed we might be in trouble, and had been watching for us. Of course we were in plenty of trouble. Without their help we would have blown over to Bellingham around midnight. We gratefully allowed them to tow us home.

Cynthia revived under a hot shower followed by a hearty bowl of freshly picked nettle soup.

I'm satisfied," she said, "We have once again had a true adventure. Gosh Les! That was just like old times!"

Lesley Crosten is an artist by day and a fiddler by night. She lives on a small green island in the Puget Sound.

Printed on recycled paper